Childrens Service

JINGLE BOY

Kieran Scott

Delacorte Press

Published by
Delacorte Press
an imprint of
Random House Children's Books
a division of Random House, Inc.
New York

Produced by 17th Street Productions,
an Alloy company
151 West 26th Street
New York, NY 10001

Visit us on the Web! www.randomhouse.com/teens

Educators and librarians, for a variety of teaching tools, visit us at
www.randomhouse.com/teachers

Cataloging-in-Publication Data is available from the Library of
Congress.

ISBN: 0-385-73113-2 (trade) 0-385-90138-0 (lib. bdg.)

The text of this book is set in 11-point Adobe Garamond.

Printed in the United States of America

September 2003

10 9 8 7 6 5 4 3 2 1

BTP

This book is dedicated to my family, but especially to my brother Ian, who would sooner perish than let a Christmas tradition die.

And, of course, to Stephanie Lane, whose beautiful brain spawned a kooky little guy named Paul.

PROLOGUE

IT WAS ONE OF THOSE PICTURE-BOOK-PERFECT WINTER nights. The kind where it's cold enough to see your breath, but not so bitter and windy that your ears start to burn. The kind where you can hold hands with your girlfriend and stroll along the salt-covered sidewalks, looking in windows and checking out Christmas decorations, without shivering and blowing into your fingers.

And for the first time in my life, I had a girlfriend to hold hands with. Not just any girlfriend, either. Sarah Saunders was the most beautiful, sweet, perfect girl in school. The girl every guy wanted. But she was mine. Mine, all mine.

"So, what do you want for Christmas?" Sarah asked, her blue eyes sparkling as we paused in front of the Gap on Ridgewood Avenue. Her cheeks were pink and her blond hair stuck out from under her white knit hat, tumbling down over her shoulders.

She squeezed my fingers and my heart went all acrobatic on me. Was she kidding? Right at that second I had everything I wanted. But I wasn't about to say that. Too cheesy. Even for me. And everyone knows that I, Paul Nicholas, can be pretty cheesy—especially at this time of year.

"Well . . . you know I want my Jeep," I said with a grin, picturing the souped-up red Cherokee I'd been begging for ever since I got my license last spring.

"*Everyone* knows you want your Jeep," Sarah said with a laugh. "Everyone knows you're getting your Jeep . . . and that it's going to have a five-disc CD changer, and a navigational system, and the hottest rims available. . . ."

Huh. Maybe bringing the catalog to school every day and showing it to all my friends had been overkill. But I couldn't help it.

"Okay, okay," I said, tilting back my head to look up at the sky as we strolled down the street. "Um . . . you could give me back my favorite sweater," I joked.

"Oh no!" she said, pointing at me. "You are never getting that one back. I love that thing. I fell asleep in it last night and wore it to bed!"

My grin widened. The thought of Sarah cuddling up in my clothes was too cool. It was such a girlfriend-type thing to do.

"All right, what do you want for Christmas?" I asked, turning the tables on her.

She stopped and looked around Ridgewood Avenue—all the brightly lit stores, some unique, like the place that sold all the African and Far Eastern art, some not so unique, like, well, the Gap. It was one of the quainter retail meccas of Bergen County. One of very few nonmall shopping experiences.

"You could pretty much get me anything and everything in this town and I'd be happy," she said, waving her mittened hand. "Seriously. I've seen something I liked in every single store we've been in."

Well, that took the pressure off. But there was no way that was going to happen. When it came time to buy something for Sarah, whatever I got was going to be amazing. Just like her.

"C'mere," I said, pulling her toward me.

She yelped, then giggled and wrapped her arms around my neck. I leaned down so that we were forehead to forehead and I could feel her breath on my face. She smelled like peppermint and freshly baked sugar cookies.

I remembered the first moment I'd seen her—the moment I'd fallen in love. It was the day our choir director, Mr. McDaniel, had handed out the Christmas carols so we could start rehearsing for the winter concert. Sarah had walked into the classroom wearing a tight red sweater, glancing around with new-girl nervousness, and I had stopped breathing. She was the most Cameron Diaz-y girl I'd ever seen in person. And then McDaniel had told her to stand next to me on the risers. All the guys in class were drooling as I shared my music with her and we started to talk. That was when the really unbelievable thing had happened.

It turned out Sarah loved Christmas just as much as I did. She loved carols, she had her own Christmas snow-globe collection, she even knew *How the Grinch Stole Christmas!* by heart, just like me. (The original cartoon in its purest form, not the psycho, acid-trip Jim Carrey version.) Every year my friends pick on me about my Christmas obsession, but here was a girl who understood—a girl who really got the fact that this was the most wonderful time of the year. She was my soul mate.

"Know what I want for Christmas?" I said as Sarah smiled up at me.

"What?" she asked.

"Mistletoe," I said. "Tons of it."

Sarah bit her lip, then stood on her toes to kiss me. And the moment our lips touched, it started to snow. I swear—at that *exact* moment. It was like something out of a Rankin/Bass Christmas special. I pulled Sarah closer, and that was when I knew. I knew it without a doubt.

This was going to be the best Christmas ever.

LAST CHRISTMAS, I GAVE
YOU MY HEART. . . .

HERE'S THE THING YOU HAVE TO UNDERSTAND: MY family has more Christmas traditions than an elf has pairs of pointy earmuffs. Most of them came from my dad's side of the family. Some of them came from my mom's. A few of them originated during my formative years as a clueless, round-faced, asthma-plagued shepherd in the church play. But each and every last one of them is sacred.

Leaving carrots out for Rudolph? Sacred.

Waking my parents up by blasting *John Denver & the Muppets—A Christmas Together* from my stereo at five A.M. every Christmas? Sacred.

Alternating tree toppers each year so that Dad gets his star and Mom gets her angel? Sacred.

Having the brightest, most elaborate, most electricity-consuming light display in Bergen County? Not just sacred, but our claim to fame. Our lights have gotten us on the Saturday-after-Thanksgiving WB11 *News at Ten* for five years running. Dad is convinced that the field reporter lives to interview us from our rooftop while we're setting up. I, however, think the woman is just addicted to Mom's hot chocolate.

But the most important tradition of all? No matter what, I have always, without question, gotten every-thing I asked for. Now, don't get me wrong, I've never abused the privilege—asked for fifty DVDs or sweaters in every color or a complete library of PlayStation games with a flat-screen TV to go with it. Nothing greedy like that. So I figured my years of responsible son-dom were ready to be cashed in. This year I had only asked for one thing. My Jeep. It's gonna be so cool, looking out my window on Christmas morning and seeing it there in the driveway, all shiny and new, with a nice huge bow on top. And once I have it, I won't have to do this anymore:

"Holly, can I have a ride to the mall?"

It was Friday afternoon, November 24, the day after Thanksgiving, and it was time for my first Christmas mall run. I was on the phone with Holly Stevenson, who has been my best friend ever since we won the water-balloon-throwing contest together at day camp. Believe it or not, she hates Christmas. She used to love it when we were kids, but for the past couple of years? Forget about it. (I know, the name is ironic, right? I mean *Holly* hates *Christmas*? It's just *wrong*.) But she does have a good reason. Her father left her and her mother two years ago *on Christmas Day* for a department store elf. You'd think that her being so anti-Noel and me being so, well, *me* would cause problems in our friendship. But hey, you don't just give up the girl who pulled you a mile and a half through the snow on a sled the day you broke your arm in three places. We manage. We just don't talk much about Christmas. Which was reason number one why asking her to come to the mall with me to shop for her least-favorite holiday was a serious risk.

Reason number two? Holly is also the only girl in my particular reality who hates malls. She buys all of her clothes at the Salvation Army store on Route 17, mainly to avoid the crowds. And here I was trying to get her to do the unthinkable—dive into Paramus Park on the biggest shopping weekend of the year.

"I'm sorry. I thought I just heard you ask me to take you to the mall," Holly said in a sugar-sweet tone. "Did someone spike your eggnog?"

"Holly—"

"Why don't you ask Marcus and Matt?" she asked.

"They're playing basketball at the Y," I told her. They'd called earlier and asked me to come, but today I was on a mission. "Besides, I want a girl's opinion."

Holly snorted.

"Come on," I said desperately. "I'll buy you waffle fries at Chick-fil-A."

"Throw in a coffee milk shake."

"You got it," I replied with a grin.

"I'll be there in ten minutes," Holly said. "And you'd better not be wearing that stupid Santa hat or the deal is off."

I looked up at the furry white rim of the chapeau in question and pulled it from my head. "I wouldn't even think of it."

After hanging up with Holly, I jogged downstairs, still clutching the hat. I just couldn't bring myself to leave the Holly-offensive accessory behind. Between Thanksgiving and Christmas, I never leave the house without it. In fact, I pretty much never leave my room without it. I honestly don't know how this habit started and believe me, I'd break myself of it if I could, but I'm a little bit OCD about the Santa hat. Whenever I try to put it away, I get this horrible, overwhelming feeling that somehow Christmas will be destroyed if I do.

I know. I should seek professional help.

I came around the corner into the kitchen to find my father leaning over the Formica table, studying the blueprints for this year's light extravaganza, tentatively titled "Santa in Space." It included a flying Santa saucer, nine NASA-outfitted reindeer, and a few aliens pieced together from costumes he'd bought at the Party City post-Halloween blowout. Yes, post-Halloween. I told you, we take this holiday seriously, and if that means planning in advance, well, that's what my father will do.

As always at this time of year, Dad was sporting an L.L. Bean flannel tucked in over a turtleneck and a pair of thick cords. His semibald head reflected the dim light from the chandelier above as he cleaned his glasses. When Dad was a kid, he wanted to be a lumberjack, but unfortunately he'd been cursed with the build of an accountant and the brain of an astrophysicist. These qualities had combined to make him the third-most-visited orthodontist in northern New Jersey.

"Hey, Dad," I said.

He looked up, startled, and knocked over his Frosty the Snowman mug full of peppermint tea. (The klutz factor may have also gotten in the way of the lumberjacking career. Of course, it's not that comforting to the metal-mouthed kids in his chair, either.) Luckily he managed to grab all of his plans before the tea lake spread too far. I quickly mopped up the mess with some paper towels.

My father took a deep breath and reverently laid out the blueprints again, smoothing down the corners. "Sorry, son," he said. "Did you say something?"

"Yeah . . . I'm going to the mall to pick up a gift for Sarah," I told him.

This got his attention.

"I like that Sarah," he said, straightening up and giving me one of those fatherly smiles. "She's got the spirit, that one."

"Yeah, she does," I said.

Sarah Saunders has now been my girlfriend for exactly twenty-eight days, ever since we had our first kiss under the mistletoe at Macy's. And it has been the best twenty-eight days of my life. I love everything about Sarah. I love the fact that she's always interested when I talk about my Jeep, even though everyone else is getting sick of it. I love the fact that she's systematically attempted to taste everything on the cafeteria menu—however unidentifiable—just to find out what she likes best. I love that she takes my varsity soccer jacket from me every morning at school and wears it around all day. There is nothing sexier than a beautiful girl wearing your clothes.

Sarah and I had been spending more time together recently because we were both on the organizing committee for the Holiday Ball. I'm in charge of decorations, and Sarah took over the Secret Santa program.

She'd spearheaded the campaign to up the maximum expenditure per student from five dollars to ten. Of course, we don't get much alone time because neither one of us has our own car . . . *yet*. Sarah can't stop talking about the fact that her boyfriend is soon going to have the hottest car at school. Her boyfriend. Me!

Anyway, last weekend she met my parents and it was great. She spent almost an hour talking with them about present buying, innovative wrapping techniques (my mom took notes), and what she expects to get from her parents for Christmas.

Okay, so her interest in the holiday veers toward the gifts, but that's okay, right? Everyone likes to get presents. And that's why I had to find something perfect for her.

"I'm gonna go outside and wait for Holly," I said as I shoved my arm through the sleeve of my ski jacket.

"I'll walk out with you," my father said, dropping his red drafting pencil. "I need to make an Island stop."

An Island stop. Code for "I need to go to Treasure Island and do some more damage to the old credit card." I swear, during the month of November my dad keeps that place in business.

In fact, all the Nicholas family Christmas craziness really comes from my father. You see, my father *loved* my grandfather. And my grandfather was kind of . . . well . . . one light short of a working strand. The man left his tree up year-round. He made toys in his basement. He had every kid in town under the age of twelve categorized as either naughty or nice.

In short, the man thought he was Santa Claus.

And while my father doesn't stray quite so far over the line, he does make sure to honor his father's memory not only by following all the old man's traditions, but by doing the whole holiday to the hilt. Why does my mother put up with it? you ask. Well, she's just a happy person in general. I'm sure if the woman could carol 365 days a year without getting arrested, she would. As for me, I grew up infected by the Christmas spirit. I know everyone around me thinks it's lame, but I happen to think it's cool in a way. It's cool to love something so purely. It's cool to keep my grandfather's memory alive. It's cool to get my face on the news every year.

If I could just kick this Santa hat habit, I'd be golden.

My father and I walked out the front door to find a dirty Taurus with New York license plates idling in front of the house. Some guy with a cigarette hanging out of his mouth rolled down the window as we approached my dad's car. His wife was behind the steering wheel and there were three, if not more, large children in the backseat who appeared to be reenacting the latest episode of *WWE SmackDown!* Limbs kept flying into view sporadically. Suddenly a pudgy freckled face was flattened up against the window before being pulled down into the fray again, leaving behind a trail of saliva.

"Hey! When do your lights go up, man?" the guy shouted over the din.

"Shut up!" his wife screeched, turning toward the backseat. "For the love of God, shut up!"

"We start tonight," my father responded calmly.

The guy muttered something under his breath and the woman now turned her venom on him. "You said they'd be up already! You *said* we'd have a nice family outing!"

The Taurus peeled out and careened down to the end of the block, where it ran the stop sign and caught a little air before coming down on the other side of the intersection. My father and I looked at each other and rolled our eyes.

"New Yorkers."

There is nothing more Christmas than the Paramus Park mall during the holiday season. Sure, there are people who would take issue with that statement—the ones who swear by the rival Garden State Plaza. Let me just say, they don't know what they're talking about. The people at the GSP do *not* know how to decorate, they stick their Santa in the most remote, most unpopulated, least Santa-worthy end of the mall so that most people can't even *find* him, and they don't play Christmas carols until the week before Christmas. Pathetic.

Paramus Park is where it's at. It's smaller, it's homier, there's tinsel everywhere, and it has a calmer, cheerful vibe. Isn't that what holiday shopping is all about?

Holly and I walked through the sliding glass doors and the second Holly's Skechers hit the linoleum, a woman carrying about fifty bags slammed right into her side and kept walking. Sometimes I really think Holly is invisible to all people over twenty-five. The girl cannot walk through a crowded place without getting constantly bombarded.

"Is it possible to suffer death by mall?" she asked through her teeth, stepping up next to me.

I smiled and shook my head at her, taking in a deep breath of the mocha-scented air. There wasn't a mall surface that hadn't been decked with ribbons, fake fir garlands, big, shiny plastic Christmas ornaments, and twinkling white lights. Registers beeped, "Joy to the World" blared over the loudspeakers, every store had replaced its regular bags with special red and green ones—this was the mall the way it was meant to be.

And soon I was going to be a part of all this. Starting next week, I was going to begin my dream job as an assistant Santa at the Paramus Park North Pole. My mother had picked up the costume for me last night and I swear, when my dad saw it, he had tears in his eyes. I couldn't wait to get started. But today I had another mission.

"Come on," I said to Holly. "It's gonna be fun. It's not like I wore the hat."

It was shoved inside the breast of my zipped-up jacket, but she didn't need to know that. "Okay, but one screaming kid steps on my foot and we're outta here," she replied, shrugging out of her long black coat.

"But I WANT it! I want it I want it I want it! I WANT it now!"

Right on cue, a mother who was clearly at the end of a very frayed rope came barreling out of K•B Toys, forcibly dragging a purple-faced child behind her. He clung with both hands to her one arm, digging his tiny Nikes into the floor. Tiny Nikes that were headed straight in Holly's direction.

I grabbed Holly and pulled her out of the kid's way.

"My hero," Holly said sarcastically, flicking her red

hair over her shoulder and turning to glare at the offenders.

"Well, maybe Santa will bring it for you," the mother suggested desperately, pulling her sleeve back up before the kid managed to strip her bare and give the line at the merry-go-round a real show.

"Santa?" the kid said hopefully. The screaming stopped. "Okay."

There it was. The magic of the big guy.

Crisis averted, the mom picked the kid up and headed for the doors.

"So, what are you getting Miss Perfect for Christmas, a lobotomy?" Holly asked, starting to walk, her coat folded over her arms.

"I don't get what your problem with Sarah is," I said, sidestepping a stroller to catch up with her. "She's always nice to you."

"She tolerates me because I intimidate her," Holly said, rolling her big green eyes.

"Why would you intimidate her?" I asked absently. I was busy scanning the stores we were passing by. Yankee Candle Company, no. Sunglass Hut, no. Bebe . . . eh . . . maybe.

"Because, moron, I'm a girl, I'm a babe, I'm your best friend," Holly said flatly. "Do the math."

I had to stop for that one. "You think she's *jealous* of you?" I asked, grinning at the ridiculousness of the idea. "You think she thinks that you and me—"

Another eye roll. Holly's face turned red beneath her freckles. "No one ever said she was intelligent."

I had to sit on the rim of one of the potted plants until I stopped laughing uncontrollably.

"Hey! It's not *that* out there," Holly said. "People have been picking on us about being a couple since the third grade."

She had me there. That was what happened when your best friend was a girl. But the thought that Sarah would take it seriously was just funny. Sarah knew she was the only girl I wanted.

"Come on," Holly said, clearly out of patience just two minutes into our trip. She swept past me into an accessories store. "There has to be something ugly and pink you can get her in here."

I caught my breath and followed Holly inside. As predicted, there was a ton of ugly pink stuff—furry headbands, huge earrings, purses shaped like boxes with pink zebra stripes. None of it exactly screamed, "Sarah!" Most of it actually screamed, "Landfill!"

"I don't think so," I said to Holly, turning to go.

"Wait! Get her this!" Holly called out.

She picked up a tiny rubber pig from the counter and squeezed it. A little rubber piece of poop squirted out of its butt and was then sucked back in. Holly laughed as she made it poop over and over and over again. My face twisted up in disgust.

"Are you even a girl?" I asked her.

"Killjoy," she said, slapping the pig back down on the counter with about twenty others that were marked down ten times. Maybe I *would* have had better luck if I'd brought Marcus and Matt.

We walked back out into the mall and a huge guy dressed in head-to-toe Jets gear rammed into Holly's shoulder and sent her spinning.

"Ow! Look where you're going, loser!" Holly shouted, gripping her arm. He didn't even turn around. She trudged over to me and we both sat down on the end of a wooden bench in the center of the mall. "I hate Jets fans," she muttered under her breath. She took one look at my profile and sighed. "You have no idea what to get her, do you?" she asked.

"None," I admitted. All I knew was that it had to be perfect. The perfect present for the perfect girl.

"I'm going to be here for the rest of my life, aren't I?" Holly added.

"Probably," I replied.

"Okay, what you need is a plan," she said. She pointed past my face toward the Sears wing. "We start at that end of the mall and we hit every single store. I don't care if it's a tobacco shop or a porn outlet, we are going everywhere. We leave no piece of chintz unturned. And if we don't find a present by the end of the day . . ."

She reached into my jacket and pulled out my Santa hat, twirling it over her head gleefully. ". . . I will eat your hat."

"How did you know it was in there?" I asked, turning beet red.

"Like you could really leave the house without it," Holly said, standing. "Now, let's go. There are at least twenty more people in this place just *waiting* to walk into me."

I stood up and followed her, my confidence in the mission renewed. Somewhere in this mall was the perfect gift for Sarah. All I had to do was find it.

OH, YOU BETTER WATCH OUT, YOU BETTER NOT CRY . . .

"PAUL! HOLLY!" MY MOM EXCLAIMED FROM BEHIND the front counter at Fortunoff. Then her face fell. "What's wrong?"

I walked up to her, folded my arms on her glass-topped counter, and collapsed. We'd been at the mall for two hours and thirty-seven minutes and I had nothing to show for it except a stomachache of Cinnabonian proportions.

"He's all malled out, the poor thing," Holly said with false sympathy, patting my back. "I told him not to get the extra icing, but does he ever listen?"

My mother laughed. She loved Holly. According to my mom, Holly had that whole "teen angst thing going on." She regarded my best friend with a sort of anthropological fascination.

"Sweetie, my manager's looking," my mother said under her breath.

"Sorry." I straightened up and tried to look like a paying customer. "What can you show me in a solid gold noose?"

"It can't be that bad," my mother said in her perpetually positive tone. "Tell me all about it." She patted my hand, then folded hers together on the counter, smiling sympathetically.

At this point, let's take a moment to appreciate my mom.

Worked on her feet all day, every day, dealing with what may be the most demanding, bitchy, jewelry-buying market in the country, yet there she stood—unwrinkled, unbroken, lipstick perfectly applied. And later she'd go home, scoff about the customers and the managers and the power-drunk mall security guy who hit on her every day ("Wanna try on my hat, little lady?"), and serve up a perfect dinner. Then tomorrow she'd get up and do it all over again. What a woman. Just looking at her made me smile.

"I can't find a present for Sarah," I said dramatically, gunning for some motherly sympathy.

"That is so not true!" Holly exclaimed. She turned to my mother, ready to make her case. "*I* have found *dozens* of perfectly good gifts for Sarah. It's your son here who—"

"Like I'm really going to get her a towel warmer," I said.

"Who doesn't like a toasty-warm towel when they get out of the shower?" Holly asked innocently.

My mother laughed again. "Well, honey, you still have a lot of time," she said. "Don't let it get you down."

"Excuse me, miss?" a guy said to my mother. "I'd like to see something in this case over here."

"I'll be right back," my mother told me before following the man around the cash register station and out of view.

I turned and pushed myself away from the counter. "I don't know, Hol, maybe I should just give up. I mean, I—"

And then I saw it. The most perfect, glittering necklace ever forged by man. Marge Horvath, one of my mom's managers, was holding it up over the counter and it caught the light from overhead, causing a spark so bright I almost had to shield my eyes. At that moment I could hear the angels singing. One flawless, heart-shaped, deep red ruby set inside a heart-shaped gold pendant. Of course! Red for Christmas! A heart for love! Could it *be* any more perfect? I could feel it in my soul. This was it. This was the gift I'd been looking for.

It was classy. It was beautiful. It was all too easy to picture it draped around Sarah's neck, dangling nice and low between her perfect—

"How much is that?" I asked Marge, taking one giant step over to her.

Marge was slightly older than my mom and had orangy tan skin, a product of the Hollywood tanning salons that have been popping up all over the place lately. I'd only met her once before and I didn't like her. She had perpetual coffee breath and the most affected smile I'd ever encountered. As I stood before her, salivating for the piece of jewelry dangling from her hand, she eyed me up and down with what could only be called disdain.

"I'm sorry, *sir.* I believe the lady was here first," she said in a nasal voice.

For the first time I noticed a slim woman with dyed-blond hair and perfectly applied eyeliner, wearing more gold jewelry than they'd had on the set of *The Mummy.* A Jersey Mall Mom. A Jersey Mall Mom who wanted my necklace.

She inched closer to the counter, pointedly ignoring me as Marge handed her the necklace. The moment her fingers touched the pendant, I had an incredible urge to deck her. She tilted back her head and looked down her nose at it.

"I'm not sure . . . ," she said.

"I am! I'm sure! I'll take it!" I exclaimed.

The woman shot me a look of death. "Excuse me, do you mind?"

Flushing, I took a step back to give her a little more space and started praying, my fingertips tapping the glass counter. *Please don't let her buy it. Please don't let her buy it. Please don't let her—*

"Paul, are you serious?" Holly asked suddenly, stepping up next to me. She stood on her toes to see over my shoulder and the woman shot her an impatient look. "After everything we've been through today, you're gonna get her *that*?"

"Yes, I am," I said to her under my breath. "It's perfection."

"All right," Holly said skeptically, raising her eyebrows. She leaned one elbow on the counter and looked up at Marge. "How much for the rock?"

"Excuse me," the Mall Mom said. "I was here first."

"Whatever, lady," Holly said dismissively. "You need another piece of jewelry like this woman needs another ten minutes on the tanning bed."

They both sucked wind. The customer's heavily ringed hand flew to her chest, while Marge's fingers fluttered toward her orange face. Once they got over their shock, they both looked out for blood.

"You're not helping!" I singsonged under my breath, smiling at the Mall Mom. I also glanced over my shoulder for my own mother. She probably wouldn't be happy with Holly insulting the customers. But she was still out of sight somewhere, helping that guy.

"Yes, I am," Holly replied.

"Look, there has to be more than one, right?" I asked, trying to be helpful.

"No," Marge answered. "This is a one-of-a-kind piece."

"We'll take it," Holly said. She reached over my shoulder and pulled the necklace right out of the Mall Mom's grasp.

"Who do you think you are?" the Mall Mom protested, hands on hips.

"Lady, aren't you late for a lip wax or something?" Holly said impatiently.

The woman turned about six shades of red, spun on her high heels, and stalked away. I made a mental note never to bring Holly to the mall again. She'd clearly hit her other-people threshold for the day.

Handing the necklace over to Marge, Holly stood up straight. "Ring this up, please," she said politely.

"You can't be serious," Marge responded, now holding the necklace away from her like a smelly diaper.

"More serious than a bad hair day," Holly said, her eyes flicking up to Marge's perfect bun.

Narrowing her eyes like a true villain, Marge slowly turned toward the cabinet to find a box for the necklace. It was at that moment that I realized I was actually going to get it. It was as good as mine!

"What's going on over here?" my mother asked, reappearing from around the cash register.

"I found something for Sarah," I told her. Marge turned and looked from me to my mother and back again.

"Marge, this is my son, Paul. You remember him," my mother said with a smile.

It was clear from Marge's stunned, slightly disgusted expression that she did not, in fact, remember me. For a split second I thought she was going to tell my mother what Holly had said to the Mall Mom, but apparently escaping from us was more important to her than tattling. She handed my mother the necklace.

"Good. Then you'll take care of this, won't you?" Marge said. "I have some bookkeeping to do."

She was gone before anyone had a chance to answer her.

"Paul, there's no way you can afford this," my mother told me gently.

Holly reached over and slid the necklace from my mother's fingers, then flipped the price tag over.

"Whoa," she said. "You sure you don't want to go back for that pig?"

I glanced at Holly. I had to admit, I didn't have a lot of disposable cash at the moment—I'd already spent most of my saved-up allowance on the ticket to the Holiday Ball, a new suit, and a red tie with the subtle outline of light strands all over it. But how much could one necklace be?

I looked at the price and gulped.

"I can afford it," I lied, my voice squeaking out. I *could* afford it. If I got an advance on my next six years' allowance, sold my entire DVD collection on eBay, started panhandling outside Neiman Marcus, and maybe sold my soul to the devil.

If I did all that *plus* took out a loan against my college fund, then yeah, no problem.

"Well . . . you get an employee discount, right?" I asked my mother in my most innocent voice.

"Ten percent. But Paul, I can't let you spend that much," she said.

"But Mom, it's perfect," I semiwhined.

"Paul—"

"It's one of a kind."

"Paul—"

"Pleeeeeeeeze?"

I'm not ashamed to admit I pulled out the big guns. I threw in the puffed-out bottom lip, the sorrowful puppy-dog eyes. I'm only human.

She took a deep breath. I had her.

"Do you even have the money to pay for this?" she asked.

Okay, so maybe *she* had *me*.

"No . . . ," I admitted. "But I will!"

"So how do you expect to pay for it now?" she asked warily.

I grinned the hopeful grin of penniless kids everywhere. "I was thinking . . . maybe . . . you could put it on your credit card and I could pay you back?"

Holly scoffed unsupportively and my mom blinked. But it wasn't like this was unheard of. I would never have gotten my dirt bike if she hadn't charged it and then waited for me to mow a summer's worth of lawns to pay her back. Which I *had*, by the way. My credit rating was golden!

"All right," she said finally, taking the necklace from Holly. She shook her head as she walked to the register. "But sweetie, I really hope you've thought about this. You've just met this girl. Are you sure she's worth it?"

"Come on, Mrs. Nick," Holly said. "You've met Sarah, right? I bet she's never in her life gone out with socks that didn't exactly match the color of her top. She deserves the love of a good man."

My mother, clearly confused, shook her head and laughed. "All right," she said. Then all I heard was the glorious sound of the register buttons beeping away. My mother swiped her Visa through the register and the transaction was complete. The necklace was mine!

"You so owe me, Nicholas," Holly said, turning around and leaning her elbows back on the counter. "You owe me big."

I smiled my agreement, but I was no longer listening. I was too busy imagining the look of elated adoration that would come over Sarah's face the moment she opened her one-of-a-kind gift. She'd wear it to the Holiday Ball. And whenever anyone asked her where she'd gotten it, she'd sigh and say, wistfully staring off, "A Christmas gift, from my boyfriend, Paul. He's not only the most handsome, talented, intelligent guy in school, but he's the best kisser in the world, he knows *American Pie* by heart, and he rides a skateboard like nobody's business. How did a girl like me get so lucky?"

This really was going to be the best Christmas ever.

*   *   *

My chin was held high and I clutched my Fortunoff bag, feeling like the sugar daddy I was. Okay, it's tough to be a sugar daddy without a car, but I *had* just laid out serious cash to buy jewels for my woman, so that was something. I was Affleck to her J.Lo. Bobby to her Whitney. Billy Bob to her Angelina.

Okay, never mind.

"God, you are such a geek," Holly said, grinning at me. "You'd think you just became the first male to give birth or something."

"Hey, give me a moment to bask in my glory, all right?"

"Fine, fine," Holly said. "Can we just get out of here already?"

As we approached the center of the mall, the crowd grew thicker, the decibel level louder. We were getting closer to the North Pole. Or the North Pole as re-created by the creative director of Paramus Park. Santa's red velvet chair was set up in front of a little "snow"-covered hut and surrounded by velvet roping. The music was louder here, but it was almost drowned out by the wails of frightened children. I never understood why some kids were afraid of Santa. According to family lore, I'd taken my first step the second I'd seen him up there waiting for me.

And now I was going to *be* Santa.

"We have to go check this guy out," I said, making my way around the fenced-off fake snow area.

"Please tell me you are not going to go sit on Santa's lap."

"Give me a little credit," I shot back. "I just want to see if they got an actual old guy instead of some zit-infected fifteen-year-old. Whoever it is will be showing me the ropes next week."

"I can't believe you're going to be Santa," Holly said as she followed me. "It's like hero worship in its purest form."

When we came around the corner of the roped-off area, my stomach clenched with disappointment. Santa was sitting on his big red velvet throne with a pudgy-faced kid on his lap. His bowl-full-of-jelly padding was convincing enough and his beard was somewhat genuine looking, but it was totally clear to me that underneath it all, the guy was not in the Santa spirit. He looked bored. And he was not ho-ho-hoing.

"Okay, I hear ya. You want a pony," he said to his knee rider. He wasn't even trying to mask his clearly adolescent voice. "But what are you going to listen to on your personal CD player while you're *riding* your pony?"

The kid gave him a blank-eyed stare, folding his fingers together in his lap.

"That's right!" Santa announced, reaching down into a box at the side of his throne. He pulled out a cheap CD jewel case and handed it to the kid. "You're gonna listen to *Santa's* favorite rapper, Scooby. Scooby is way cool. And this is his first album! All ya gotta do is ask your mom to give me nine ninety-nine plus tax and you can listen to Santa's favorite music!"

The kid's eyes grew bright. He jumped off Santa's lap and ran off, waving the CD above his head. "Mom! Mom! I need nine ninety-nine plus tax!"

"I feel physically ill," I said flatly, my arms suddenly hanging at my sides like deadweight. I couldn't believe this guy was using his position as Santa to hawk what was undoubtedly his own bad rap album. "We have to report this."

"To who? The North Pole police?" Holly asked. She reached out and tugged on my arm. "Come on, let's get out of here. When you're up there being Santa next week, you can uncorrupt all the kids he corrupted."

"All right," I said, trying to see Holly's bright side. She was right. I'd be such a great Santa I'd put this guy to shame. "Let's get out of here before you burst a blood vessel."

Holly actually took a skip of joy as we headed for the car. She could be pretty cute when she wasn't paying attention.

"Hey, can I get my hat?" I asked as we approached the short hallway that led to the door.

Holly stopped dead in her tracks and I felt my heart plummet. "I don't have your hat," she said, turning ever so slowly to face me.

"Yes, you do," I said. My whole body started to heat up. "You took it, remember? What did you do with it?"

Holly stuffed her hands in her coat pockets, but it clearly wasn't in there. It was too big to fit in there.

"You lost it?" I said loudly. "How could you lose my hat?"

"I'm sorry!" Holly said, her face paler than usual. "I must have put it down in one of the four thousand stores you dragged me into."

"Hey! Going to every store was *your* idea, remember?" I said, feeling desperate. I looked around at the floor, hoping she'd just now dropped it and hadn't noticed.

"Come on, Paul," Holly said placatingly. "It's not like it's irreplaceable. I'll buy you a new one right now."

She took a step in the direction of the North Pole, where all the Christmas stands were. I didn't budge. And I didn't say a word. How was I supposed to explain my superstition to her? She knew I always wore the hat, but I'd never told anyone about my little obsession—the fact that I knew in my bones that Christmas wouldn't be Christmas without it.

My Santa hat. The one with the semimatted fur around the headband. The one with the pom-pom that was stained with hot chocolate and was hanging on by a few short threads. The one that still smelled like mulberry wine from the time my mom left that Christmas candle burning in my room. It *was* irreplaceable.

"No. Forget it," I said, forcing a smile. "I just want to get home and wrap Sarah's present."

"There ya go! Focus on that!" Holly said, relaxing. "You found the perfect gift."

As we turned toward the door again, I took a deep breath and told myself to chill. Maybe it was all going to be okay. Maybe this had happened for a reason. I had Sarah now. I no longer needed my hat to make Christmas perfect.

I was just starting to feel a bit better when I caught a flash of red out of the corner of my eye. When I got a closer look, my jaw dropped.

"Ugh! That is just wrong!" Holly said, grimacing.

Apparently Santa had decided to take a break after making his last sale. He was standing next to the glass doors to the parking lot making out with . . . no . . . practically *mauling* some girl right around the corner from K•B. If any of the kids pouring out of there saw him, they could be traumatized for life. *This* was the guy who was supposed to train me to be the universal symbol of Christmas itself? I was about to walk up to him and give that sorry excuse for a Saint Nick a piece of my mind when the couple shifted and I got a good look at Santa's conquest.

"Oh my God," Holly said.

My knees went out from under me as all of my daydreams flashed before my eyes in a sickening Technicolor whirl. Sarah and I making snow angels, Sarah and I singing carols, Sarah and I opening gifts by the fire.

Sarah with her lipstick smeared by some scraggly loser in a cheap Santa suit. No, wait, that was reality.

"Paul? Are you okay?" Holly said. I saw a flash of tongue between Sarah and Santa and my stomach lurched. "Okay, that's enough. Turn around. Don't look."

But I couldn't make myself move. Instead I closed my eyes, said a little prayer to the mercy gods, and opened them again, but the nightmare hadn't disappeared. It was all too true. My girlfriend was being publicly groped . . . by jolly old Saint Nick.

The next few minutes passed in a blur. Sarah suddenly opened her eyes, saw me, and managed to push Scooby or whatever the heck his name was away from her. I think I said something. Her name, maybe. Maybe just the word *what.* She looked down at the floor for a second, clearly ashamed, but when she looked up again, her whole beautiful face had hardened with resolve.

"I'm sorry you had to find out this way, Paul," she said, her voice light and sweet and not sorry at all. "I'm with Scooby now."

"*This* is your boyfriend?" Santa said, his bushy white eyebrows lifting. "Dude, no wonder you came after some Scooby lovin'."

I felt like I was melting inside my several layers of clothing. "Sarah, how long . . . ?"

She took a few steps over to me and laid her hands on my chest. "We got involved too fast," she said, her big blue eyes seeming to mock me. "I just moved here. I need to see what's out there. And besides, Scooby's older. He has a car. He has a career. He's going to be a famous rapper."

At that point Scooby came up next to her and slipped his arm around her back, lifting his fake-whiskered chin. Sarah smiled up at him.

"He bought me this coat to celebrate his CD release," Sarah said, drawing the soft red wool more closely around her. "Isn't that so sweet?"

This wasn't happening. She wasn't actually breaking my heart in the middle of a mall and expecting me to be happy for her, was she? Didn't I mean anything to her? Didn't she know how much I cared?

"Come on, Paul," Holly said, stepping in front of me so that I had to stop staring pathetically at Santa and his new Mrs. Claus. "Come on, let's get the hell out of here. You don't need this Barbie, anyway."

I turned slowly, my head pounding so hard it felt like my skull was expanding. Scooby laughed behind me and it made me feel about three feet tall. A few hours ago I'd entered this mall with the most amazing girlfriend in the world and about a thousand expectations for the perfect Christmas to come.

I was leaving it hopeless, penniless, and girlfriendless. And I knew exactly why.

I'd lost my Santa hat.

Christmas was falling apart before my eyes.

I'm Gettin' Nuttin' for Christmas . . .

"ARE YOU CATATONIC?" HOLLY ASKED.

I wasn't exactly sure, but if catatonic meant sitting in a vinyl booth, barely able to breathe, definitely unable to move, with your brain filled with something that felt like oatmeal, then I guess I was. Unsure of what to do with me, Holly had driven from the mall to the Suburban Diner and somehow gotten me out of the car and into a booth. (The only thing I could recall from the walk through the parking lot was the puddle I'd stepped in, leaving my left sock and sneaker very wet and very cold.) There must have been a couple of kids sitting at the table behind me because there was a lot of banging and kicking and moving around and every once in a while I would bounce forward when a limb hit the back side of my seat particularly hard.

The one time Sarah and I had gone to the movies together, the kids behind us had spent the first ten minutes of the flick talking and kicking and wrestling. I'd told them to quiet down and they had—for about five seconds—and then they got even louder. I was just about to lose it when Sarah turned around and bribed them into silence with her jumbo bag of plain M&M's. I was so impressed with her that night, I'd fallen in love with her all over again. We spent the rest of the movie scrunched down in our seats, cuddled together, feeding each other popcorn. I couldn't believe I was never going to get to do that again.

I stared down at the congealing cheeseburger and onion rings Holly had ordered for me and tried to make sense of what had happened.

The door of the diner opened, letting in a shot of cold air, and my scalp tingled and tightened. My hat. This was all because of my Santa hat. Why had I ever taken it off?

"Eat something," Holly said.

The only part of her within my line of vision was her hand on the table, clutching her water glass. There was a wet ring on her paper place mat—the one that broke down how to make every cocktail in existence, copies of which had been lifted by half the teenagers in Bergen County. For some reason I was mesmerized by that water ring as I listened to Holly munching on her fries.

"Paul?" she said. Her hands started waving in front of my face. "Paaaw-*allll*!"

I knew I had to say something or do something to prevent her from calling up the Bergen Medical Center and having them prepare my padded room, so I mustered all my energy, took a deep breath, and said, "How . . . ?"

"I'll tell you how," Holly said, not missing a beat. "She's a backstabbing, lying little . . ."

Holly trailed off. She tries not to swear or use slurs of any kind unless she really, really has to. But I knew what she was thinking. Part of me wanted to defend Sarah's honor, but arguing with Holly takes up too much energy and I almost never win. Unless she lets me.

"I thought she cared about me," I mumbled, slumping even farther until my butt was almost dangling in thin air. My shoulder blade pressed into a hard coil in the back of the seat, but I didn't slide over. It was all just part of my misery.

"She used you," Holly stated matter-of-factly, shoving a french fry into a huge mound of ketchup on her plate. I couldn't help noticing that Holly seemed to be taking my shattered heart in stride. She'd already devoured half her chicken fingers and at least three mozzarella sticks. But then, she'd never been Sarah's number one fan.

"But . . . I'm in love with her," I said.

Holly's hand dropped to the table, french fry and all. "Come on. Seriously?"

I managed to lift a shoulder.

"You barely *know* her. She just *moved* here," Holly blurted out, her eyes wide and disbelieving. "She could be a closet speed freak, a pathological liar . . . a . . . a Britney Spears fan! How can you be in love with her?"

"You wouldn't understand," I said, shifting in my seat. As long as I'd known her, Holly had only ever had a crush on one guy—that actor Seth Green. And she dropped that when she found out he was about five inches shorter than she is. She has never—not once—mentioned an even remote interest in any of the guys at school.

"No. I guess I wouldn't," Holly replied. She popped the fry into her mouth.

"Besides, what the heck would she be using me for?" I asked, poking around for some kind of weakness in her argument. One speck of hope that maybe this whole Scooby thing was just a momentary lapse of sanity. I had to keep believing.

Holly took a long, deep breath and shot me a look. An I-know-something-you-don't-know-and-I-don't-want-to-tell-you-what-it-is look. My heart took a nosedive.

"What?" I asked, my voice full of dread.

"Nothing. Forget it," Holly said, yanking a napkin out of the dispenser at the end of the table. She made a big show of wiping off her fingers, going at each one as if she were about to perform heart surgery. Maybe she was. I mean, from her tone it seemed like she might be about to tear my still-beating heart right out of my chest.

"Oh no," I said. I pushed my hands into the seat at my sides and sat up straight, causing a cacophony of creaks, squeaks, and vinyl farts. My morbid curiosity was definitely getting the better of me. What did she *know*? "You have to tell me. You can't violate the Pact."

"The Pact states that you cannot begin a sentence and then refuse to end it," Holly pointed out, flicking her red hair over her shoulder. "I did not start any sentence. I merely gave you a look."

"Yeah, a loaded look," I said. I was starting to sweat. "Spill, Holly. Come on."

"All right, all right." She pushed her plate aside and leaned her forearms on the table, bringing her face close to mine. Her expression was placating, sorrowful, almost pitying. The kind of look you give a kid when you're about to tell him that his dog was hit by a bus. "In the locker room before gym the other day, Lainie Lefkowitz asked Sarah how things were going with you." Holly fixed her green eyes on my face, trying to discern whether or not it was safe to continue.

I tried to keep my face as expressionless as possible. "Uh-huh."

Holly took another deep breath. I stared at the smiley face pattern of the freckles just above her nose.

"She said, 'Well, at least he's getting a cool car,'" Holly said, pitching her voice a few octaves higher to imitate Sarah's. Then she let out this loud, affected giggle that sounded nothing at all like my girlfriend. Sorry. Ex-girlfriend.

I blinked. "What's so bad about that?" I asked. "I *am* getting a cool car! And Sarah was the only one who would even listen to me talk about it anymore!"

"That just proves my point! The car was *all* she cared about!" Holly exclaimed, flopping back in her seat. "She's totally materialistic!"

"Well . . . so am I," I protested feebly. "At least when it comes to my Jeep, I am." Chalk it up to one of the most pointless arguments ever devised by man or teenager.

"Whatever. All I know is, she's not good enough for you," Holly replied, shaking her head and picking up another fry. "You can do *so* much better."

"Better than Sarah?" I said. "What are you on? She's ten times too good for me. I mean, have you not *seen* her?"

Holly blew out an exasperated breath and grabbed the ketchup bottle. "She's not *that* pretty."

I wasn't even going to dignify that with a response. Maybe Holly couldn't see how perfect Sarah was because she's a girl, too. I mean, it's not like I ever grasped the Seth Green attraction. But trust me, Sarah was the most beautiful girl in my class. The day she walked through the doors at Paramus Park High, she blew away any hopes Danielle Booth had of winning "Best Looking" in the yearbook poll. And Danielle had a lock on it since the fourth grade when she was the first girl to . . . *mature,* if ya know what I mean.

Yep. Sarah was perfect. And I was supposed to be taking her to the Holiday Ball. I felt sick every time I thought about it, which was about every five seconds. The totally detail-oriented daydream I had of walking into the twinkle-lighted gym with Sarah on my arm in a slinky red dress and every guy in the room turning to stare in awe had now been obliterated by a cheesy guy with lousy tongue control in an unconvincing fat suit.

"Scooby," I said quietly, seeing his arm around Sarah's shoulders, his skinny little lips on hers, the way he'd hitched up his Santa pants before walking over to us. Of course he'd done that behind Sarah's back. If only she'd seen him. Maybe she would have—

"Do you think he'll take Sarah to the ball in the Mystery Machine?" Holly laughed.

"Do you think she's going to bring him?" I blurted out, my stomach clenching all over again. Holly arched her eyebrows at me as if this were the most obvious assumption in the world. "I mean . . . he's definitely older. . . . Do you think he'll want to come to a high school dance?"

Even as I asked this question, I knew how stupid it

was. Scooby seemed like the exact brand of all-day-Sega-playing, still-got-a-Carmen-Electra-poster-on-his-walls, I-never-got-over-high-school loser that would *love* to come to a high school dance. Especially with a girl like Sarah on his arm.

"He'll probably try to sell his CD there," Holly said with a snort.

The waitress walked over and slapped the check on our table.

"Come on. I'll take you home," Holly said, grabbing up the little slip of paper.

Home. Yes. That would be good. All I wanted to do at that moment was lie down on my bed, stare at the ceiling, and wonder where it all went wrong.

Not that there was really any doubt. None of this would have happened if I hadn't agreed to take off my hat—if Holly hadn't *made* me take off my hat and then lost it on me. But I couldn't be mad at her. I didn't even have the energy for that. Besides, I could have gotten it back from her right at the start. I just . . . hadn't tried hard enough. And now it was gone.

My Santa hat was somewhere on the grimy mall floor right now, being kicked around by holiday shoppers and flattened by baby strollers. It was all perfectly clear, to me, at least. I was being punished by Christmas.

"Oh no," I said when Holly pulled her VW Beetle to a stop at the foot of my driveway.

The transformation had begun. Boxes and crates of lights were lined up along the front path, each neatly labeled with a red or green Magic Marker. There were ladders strategically placed all around our two-story house and my dad's elaborate harness-and-pulley mechanism was already fixed around the chimney. He'd even managed to outline all the front windows with lights already. I squeezed my eyes shut. How could I have forgotten?

Holly leaned across my lap and looked up through my window. "Where's Father Christmas?" she asked. She'd been calling my dad that for as long as I could remember. Once she renounced the holiday, I thought we'd never hear it again, but she hadn't stopped using it, which was good. My father's kind of proud of the title.

"He's probably around back," I said. I couldn't believe the intense aversion I was feeling to the whole process of light stringing. All I could think about at that moment was getting inside before my father emerged from the backyard and roped me into helping. There was no way I was going to be able to get up there and be all holly and jolly with the sucking chest wound I had in my heart area.

"I'd better go," I said, yanking on the door handle.

"Oh . . . well, call me if you need to vent," Holly said as I scrambled out of the car.

"Yeah, thanks," I replied. I slammed the door behind me and strode up the driveway, clutching my Fortunoff bag. My utterly pointless, exorbitantly expensive Fortunoff bag. I had just about made it to the front door when I heard the whir of the pulley and climbing ropes and my father suddenly appeared beside me, falling out of the sky and stopping right at eye level like Spider-Man on a strand of web.

"Hi, son!" he said brightly. He bounced a couple of times, then settled, hanging there in his harness with his prescription ski goggles on and a pencil stuck behind his red-from-the-cold ear.

"Hey, Dad," I replied, hand on the doorknob.

"Get on your gear and come on out," my father said, all smiles. "I can't wait to get this puppy up and running."

"Yeah . . . I don't know, Dad," I said, my chest heavy with guilt. I looked away as his face fell. "I . . . uh . . . I guess I ate too much at the mall and I'm . . . not really feeling that well."

"Oh," my father said. There has never been one syllable filled with more disappointment. "Well, then take a rest and see how you feel. I've got some more preliminary stuff to do, anyway."

"Great," I said.

I slipped inside and closed the door, feeling like the worst son in the Western Hemisphere. I trudged up to my room, passing under the mistletoe that hung at the bottom of the stairs and the photographs from Christmases past that lined the wall along the steps. My father's disappointment and shock were no surprise. After all, I'd begged for him to let me help him my entire young life until sixth grade, when he finally decided I was old enough to be strapped to our roof. Creating the lights extravaganza was always my favorite task of the year.

But what did I care about lights at that moment? I'd just lost the girl of my dreams. And I owed my mother more money than I'd ever seen in my lifetime.

I walked into my room and dropped the Fortunoff bag on my desk by the window, right on top of the minutes from our last Holiday Ball meeting. There was a lump in my throat the size of an orange. I pulled out the little silver box, pushing the receipt back down into the bag. I took out the pendant and chain, holding it up against the waning sunlight. It swung from my fingers, glittering delicately. Sarah would have loved it.

Suddenly I felt very, *very* sorry for myself.

Wrapping the thin chain around my hand, I dropped down on top of my bedspread and lay flat on my back, staring up at the stucco ceiling. I held the hand with the pendant over my heart and took a deep breath. I heard my father trudging around overhead and tried to make myself smile. It was Christmas. The lights were going up. On Tuesday, I was going to be Santa!

But on Monday, I was going to have to spend the whole day at school with everyone knowing that Sarah had dumped me. And on Tuesday afternoon, I was going to have to spend hours at the mall being Santa-trained by the dreaded Scooby.

Maybe I could go out and get run over by a reindeer. At least it would put me out of my misery.

"Misfit! Misfit! Misfit!"
Where is that coming from? A thousand little Alvin the Chipmunk voices chant inside my head. I whirl around in the darkness. I'm surrounded by trees, but they're not like trees at all. Each one is like a series of green triangles stacked on top of one another, with plops of snow on them that look like melted Marshmallow Fluff. Something zooms by me to my right with a swoosh! leaving two tiny razor tracks in the snow. A sled. And the voices grow louder.
"Misfit! Misfit! Misfit!"
It's cold. There's a light in the distance. And suddenly,

over the hill, an army appears. An army of blue-suited elves.

And they're not just any elves, they're the tiny, goateed, big-headed clay elves from Rudolph the Red-Nosed Reindeer. They're chanting, pumping their ball-shaped hands, and carrying flickering torches as they approach me. "Misfit! Misfit! Misfit!"

I can't move. I'm too scared. What's happening? Why have the jolly little elves turned on me? They form a circle around me, raising their torches high and continuing their chant.

"Misfit! Misfit! Misfit!"

Suddenly something cold and wet, jagged and hard, hits me on the side of the face. My eye feels like it's going to explode from the pain. I look down, my vision blurred, to see the Snowman—Burl Ives's narrator snowman—shake his umbrella angrily up at me, his choppy little eyebrows coming together over his eyes.

"You don't belong here, Paul!" he shouts. "You're a reject. Sarah dumped you for a scraggly loser! You don't belong at the North Pole!"

"But . . . but I . . ."

It's no use. The snowballs start coming fast and furious, pelting me from all sides. I raise my hands to protect my face and fall to my knees. The little dentist elf stalks through the snow toward me, brandishing his tooth-pulling pliers, the ones that left the Abominable Snowman smacking his gums.

"No!" I shout. "Don't!"

"You're a bigger misfit than I ever was," Rudolph's voice says in my ear.

I look up through the shower of snowballs to find the most famous reindeer of all sneering at me from his position

at the front of Santa's team. They take off into the night,
Santa waving and calling out through all the horrible
noise, "Ho! Ho! Ho! Merry Christmas!"

And the elves start to throw their torches at me.
Closer and closer . . . I can feel the heat burning at my
face. . . .

"No!" I shout out in vain. "This was supposed to be
the best Christmas ever! Nooooo . . . !"

"Paul? Paul! For heaven's sake, wake up! *Paul!*"

My eyes wrenched open as my mother shook me
in my bed and I woke up instantly, bathed in a hot,
hot sweat. The sounds of a crackling fireplace filled my
senses, along with the scent of smoking wood. My
eyes rolled wildly around in my head, trying to find
the source of the eerie yellow-orange light that filled
my room. And then I saw them—the flames licking at
the outside of my bedroom windows.

"The roof is on fire!" my mother shouted, her face
bright pink and her hair clinging to her sweat-
drenched forehead. She had a streak of flour across her
nose. She stood up straight, clinging to her messy
apron. "Paul! Your father!"

I sprang out of bed, shoving the necklace, which
was still wrapped around my hand, into my pocket.
At first I couldn't believe what I was seeing. But then
I heard a siren in the distance and it snapped me into
the here and now. A flame suddenly came to life in
the corner of my room and started traveling toward
the floor. My father was dangling outside my window,
his head tipped back, his arms swinging at unnatural
angles behind him.

"Dad!" I shouted. I jumped onto my bed and flipped the lock on my window. My mother was hysterical now, sobbing and gasping for breath. I reached out my hand into the cold night air and grabbed at my father, wrapping my fingers around the harness that circled his upper thigh. I swung him toward me, hearing the roar of the fire outside and behind me grow louder and louder.

"Mom! I need your help!" I shouted as I wrestled with the unwieldy bulk of my deadweight father, trying to pull him through the window. The fire was spreading across the front wall of my bedroom.

Don't let him be dead, don't let him be dead, don't let him be—

My mother climbed up onto the bed next to me, wailing, and helped me drag my dad's limp form through the window. I held his weight, supporting him with my knee, as my mom undid his safety harness. I yanked off his goggles and looked down at his face as she worked, searching for a sign of life. He was so pale he looked like a ghost of himself, and his lips were turning blue.

"Dad! Dad! Wake up!" I said, slapping him a few times on the cheeks as I'd seen done in so many movies. Nothing. Not even a blink.

The latch finally came undone in my mother's shaky fingers. As we lowered him onto my bed, a burst of flame came to life just above my desk, crawling across my room and up to the ceiling.

"We have to get him out of here," I said, my voice sounding inexplicably strong. "You get his legs, I'll get his arms."

My mother grasped his ankles, holding them on

either side of her body, and started to back out of the room. I held my dad under his armpits, and his torso hung limply between us, like a hammock full of rocks. We got downstairs awkwardly but quickly and toddled our way toward the front door. I backed up to it, picked up my foot, and kicked it as hard as I could. The wood splintered and the door flew open. My mother and I ran down the walk and across the lawn, finally laying my father down on the dying brown grass near the curb. A fire engine skidded around the corner, sirens blaring, lights blazing, and screeched to a stop behind us.

"Oh, Paul, he's not . . . ?" my mother said, kneeling next to my dad. She reached out to touch him but then pulled back her hand. "Is he dead?"

I didn't want to know. I didn't want to find out. But I bent over my father's mouth and listened. There was his breath, shallow and slow, but there.

"He's breathing," I said, relieved.

"Oh, thank God!" My mother collapsed on my father's chest, clinging to him like Scarlett O'Hara in *Gone with the Wind.* (Mom made me watch it in the fifth grade.)

I tore my eyes away and looked up at my house. My house that apparently wasn't going to be there much longer. The entire roof was engulfed in flames and the second floor wasn't faring much better. The firemen shouted orders to one another and before long, a wide stream of water was blasted at the house, a couple of skinny guys not much older than me struggling with the dancing hose.

"What do we got here?" an EMT asked, seemingly appearing out of nowhere and dropping to the ground beside my mother. I looked around me for the first time and noticed that there were now three fire trucks, an ambulance, a few police cars, and a nice-sized crowd of neighbors gathered on the street.

"He's unconscious," she said as the EMT unpacked his bag. He slipped on a stethoscope and checked my father's heartbeat.

"Any idea what happened?" he asked, his slick black hair gleaming in the light from the fire.

"I . . . I was in the kitchen baking and the lights flickered," my mother said. "There was this loud buzzing sound, then a pop, and then I heard him shout."

"Sounds like he may have been electrocuted," the EMT said.

"Electrocuted?" my mother wailed.

"'Scuse me, kid!"

Dazed and light-headed, I stepped out of the way as two more emergency workers jogged through with a gurney and placed it beside my father. In a few minutes they had lifted him up and strapped him down and were loading him into an ambulance. I watched all of this happening in a sort of detached, spectatorly way, as if it were happening to someone on *ER*.

My mother beckoned to me from the back of the ambulance to get in, but I turned away from her. The fire was really quite mesmerizing. There was my room, going up in smoke and flame. Strands of Christmas lights dangled from the eaves. The Christmas wreath from the front door had flown off when I'd kicked the door down and it lay on the ground, a few tiny flames dancing around it.

"Oh, jeez, would you look at that," someone said behind me.

My eyes traveled up from the sad-looking wreath and fell on Santa in his little flying saucer, his arm raised in a wave just like the Santa in my dream. As we watched, the flames took poor Santa, first melting the ship out from under him, then crawling up his body and pulling at his face. I couldn't tear my eyes away as he morphed from the cherry-cheeked, twinkle-eyed jolly old Saint Nick into a sadistic painted clown, laughing maniacally down at me from above.

Misfit! Misfit! Misfit!

"Christmas really is punishing me," I whispered.

"Paul! Paul!" Holly's voice penetrated my descent into madness. "You're okay!" she shouted. She shoved her way past a couple of policemen and hit me with the force of an avalanche, nearly knocking me over as she hugged me.

"Ugh! You're okay!" Her hands whacked at my back as she clung to me.

When she pulled away, I could tell she'd been crying. Her whole face was white except for her very red nose.

"Come on," she said, tugging at my arm. "We have to go. We'll follow the ambulance."

The ambulance. Right. My father. Right. What the hell was wrong with me? There were more important things than my stupid house and a melting Santa. I finally turned away from Santa and his spaceship, now a widening puddle of plastic goo on what was left of my roof.

Voices whispered as the crowd parted around Holly and me.

"That poor family . . ."

"And at this time of year . . ."

"They have more Christmas spirit than the rest of us combined. It's just a shame. . . ."

Suddenly I heard a tremendous crash and the spectators gasped, inching a bit farther away from my house. I didn't even look back to see what had happened, but as I ducked into the car, a little kid hid his face in the folds of his father's coat, sniffling.

"Santa must be dead," he said sorrowfully, his red mittens clasping his father's leg.

I couldn't help agreeing.

SANTA BABY, I WANT A YACHT AND REALLY THAT'S NOT A LOT

MY HOUSE LOOKED LIKE A PIECE OF ROTTING FRUIT. There was this big, black, gooey, bubbly, smoky hole in the top right side of it that made me think of the mushy spot on an otherwise perfect apple. We had been at the hospital for a few hours and most of the firemen had packed it in and gone home, but two large guys with soot-blackened faces met Holly's car when we drove up. One of them had a clipboard. Neither of them looked very happy. I could relate.

"I don't want to go in there," I said from the backseat of the Bug.

"Paul, just remember, your father is going to be okay. Focus on that," my mother said. But her face had gone whiter and whiter the closer Holly pulled to the house. She was holding herself together by a very skinny, fraying thread. My mother rarely, if ever, lost it. And when she did, it wasn't pretty. Like the time I, purely by accident, drove her car into the pond at Van Saun Park? I really thought she was going to pop a vital organ. I hoped tonight didn't turn out like that night had, because if she lost it, I was definitely going to freak. And without my father around to be all level-headed, we'd be in serious trouble.

Mom climbed out and started to talk with the firemen. I took my dear sweet time hoisting myself out of the low backseat. I was in wallow mode. I'll be the first to admit it. Yes, it was true, my dad was going to be okay. He woke up at the hospital and even managed to tell a joke or two. ("The good news is, we won't need a tree this year—you can just plug *me* in!") But his body had been through a major trauma and he couldn't move without pain. The doctors predicted it would take at least two weeks for him to recover.

Two weeks. That was half of December. Practically the whole Christmas season. Things would not be the same without my father around. But who was I kidding? Things weren't going to be the same any way you looked at it. My house was barbecue. Blackened *Cajun* barbecue.

"We'd like to take you inside and show you the damage, ma'am," the taller, older fireman said, attempting a polite smile. He had a bushy white mustache that had turned gray from all the ash, and his light blue eyes seemed tired.

Mom started up the walk between the two firemen and Holly stepped up beside me.

"That can't be good," I said, staring at the dent in the house where my room used to be. Beams and boards jutted out of the roof at unnatural angles, and one of my windows was just not there anymore. I couldn't even imagine what it looked like inside.

Tonight my mother's favorite saying—"Paul, your room looks like a bomb hit it!"—had somehow come true.

"Look at it this way," Holly said, shoving her hands into the back pockets of her jeans. "At least now you can redecorate!"

I snorted. It was a valiant stab, but all it did was bring home the worst part of this whole thing. "Let's get this over with," I said. Then I somehow made myself start walking.

The front doorjamb was ripped and splintered where I'd kicked open the door earlier, but other than that, the downstairs was okay. Aside from the muddy footprints of about a thousand boots, everything was intact. The kitchen was a wreck, but only because my mother had been baking when the fire started. A cookie sheet with uncooked blobs of dough sat on top of the stove, and the counters were covered with spilled flour, eggshells, and various bottles, boxes, and bags of ingredients. Even in her panic my mother had managed to turn off the oven.

"Cookie?" Holly asked, walking over to the cooling rack and picking up a Toll House. My stomach grumbled noisily. It had been a long night without food. But I didn't think I was going to be able to digest.

"Go ahead," I told her. After all, she was starving, too. We'd be better off if at least one of us wasn't delirious with hunger. Holly popped the cookie in her mouth and grabbed a handful more.

The floor overhead creaked and I could hear the muffled voices of my mother and the firemen. They were in my parents' room, just above us. I glanced at

Holly. I really didn't want to go up there. But there was no point in avoiding the inevitable. Holly smiled reassuringly, her cheek sticking out from a full mouth. We headed for the stairs.

It was a nightmare. My palms were sweating and my heart was pounding so hard it was nearly choking me as I climbed the stairs. I really felt like I must be asleep and that at any second I would sit up straight in my bed, realizing it was all just a product of my twisted imagination. But when I got to the top of the stairs, the first thing I saw was the miniature Christmas tree my mom and I had made when I was in kindergarten, toppled to the floor in front of the hallway table where it once sat. It was smashed and stepped on, the mini-Santa and snowman ornaments ground into the rug like tiny crushed corpses.

When I didn't wake up from seeing that heinous sight, I knew for sure that I wasn't dreaming.

Holly and I stood at the top of the stairs as my mother and the two firemen walked over to my bedroom. My mother gasped and her hand flew to her mouth.

"Mom?" I said.

She looked at me with this dazed, horrified expression, then stepped into the room ahead of me to make space for me to get through. I kind of wished she hadn't.

I had never seen anything like it. It wasn't my room. It couldn't be.

"It's pretty bad," the fireman's low voice rumbled.

The wall had collapsed on top of my bed, engulfing it in a pile of . . . well . . . *crap*. Wood, paper, plaster, roof shingles—all soaked and pungent—tumbled over the mattress and onto the floor. Everything was wet. Water dripped from the ceiling, ran from the window-sills onto the floor. When I stepped on my wall-to-wall carpeting, water bubbled up from under my feet and chilled the canvas of my sneakers. I pulled my sweater closer to me. You could see the stars through the gaping hole in the upper corner of the room.

I tore my eyes away from the bed and made the mistake of looking at my desk. The wallpaper had peeled all around it and hung down in limp strips. My computer screen was covered with hardened bubbles and the CDs that always littered the surface of the desk had *become* the surface. They had melted and congealed to the desk in pools of psychedelic colors. My schoolbooks were charred and soaked and there was a pile of black ash that had once been a stack of notebooks.

And the smell. Ugh. I can't even describe it. The usually comforting scent of burned wood mixed with this acrid, sour aroma that came from melted synthetics—plastics of all kinds that I never even realized I owned. I took a step toward the desk.

"Son, you don't want to go over by the window."

I ignored him. I had to see if there was anything salvageable. I *lived* on my desk. Almost everything that mattered was over there.

"Paul," my mother said in a half-pleading, half-warning tone.

The floor squeaked and creaked under me, but I barely noticed. My hand was reaching out for the framed picture of Sarah and me that sat next to the keyboard. It was melted and crinkled and distorted. I almost wanted to cry when I saw it. It was the final nail in the coffin. Not only had I lost the girl, I'd lost the only photographic proof I had that the girl had ever been mine.

Maybe I could get some of those pictures Naho Nakasaki had taken for the yearbook at the last Holiday Ball meeting. Maybe she still had the negatives. If I could just get my hands on—

But then, what did it matter? Sarah had dumped me, right? Why did I want to remember what I couldn't have?

"Come on, honey," my mother said, stepping up next to me and putting her hands on my shoulders. "You can sleep in the den downstairs tonight and tomorrow we'll figure out how to fix this mess."

"Okay," I said in a daze.

I didn't want to be here anymore, anyway. It was too depressing. Ripped posters hung from their tacks, the totem pole from our trip to Arizona was tipped over and broken in half, my soccer uniform lay dirty and scorched atop my collapsing hamper. That morning I'd woken up all happy-go-lucky in this very room, and now it was destroyed. Just like I had been that afternoon by Sarah.

It would've been almost poetic if it hadn't sucked so very, very badly.

As I turned to go, I caught a glimpse of something out of the corner of my eye. There, on the sopping wet floor, trampled and ripped and deteriorating, was a crushed silver Fortunoff bag.

"No," I said under my breath.

I dropped to the ground, tossing the frame aside,

and picked up the bag. The whole bottom fell out, landing with a wet *thwack* on top of a twisted piece of fabric that used to be my favorite boxers. I sifted through the mottled paper and found the receipt, now nothing but a gobbed-up spitball. When I tried to unfold it, it disintegrated in my hands. Sitting in my pocket was a piece of jewelry intended for the girl I loved who could not care less about me. A piece of jewelry that I couldn't afford. And I was stuck with it for the rest of my life.

I couldn't have been more screwed.

"Wicked cool!" Marcus Seiler said, stepping into my bedroom. He pulled the hood on his sweatshirt up to cover his gelled hair against the cold, then bobbed his head as he surveyed the damage. He sniffed and made a disgusted face. "It stinks in here, man."

Yeah, dude. That would be because of the massive fire. "I know," I told him.

"Did you take pictures yet?" Matt Viola asked as he hovered by the door. He looked at the floor warily and decided not to take the risk of actually entering the destruction zone.

"Didn't think of that," I told them, resisting the urge to punch something. Didn't they get that this sucked? They were acting like I'd torched the room myself—for fun. They might be my friends, but sometimes they weren't all that bright.

"You totally should," Matt said.

Yeah, I thought. *I'll get right on that.* There was a rumble and a crash in my closet and Marcus jumped halfway across the room.

"What the heck was that?" he asked.

"Squirrel," I replied. "He moved in sometime last night. Scared the crap out of me this morning when I came up to get my cell."

"Cool," Matt said. "Get a picture of that, too."

Marcus and I just looked at him for a second; then Marc clapped. "We're making a Mickey-D's run," he said. "Wanna come?"

"No thanks," I said as I followed them back downstairs. I hadn't told them about Sarah yet and if they stayed here for five minutes longer, I knew they were going to ask about her. I wasn't ready to deal with questions and the obvious comments. ("But *dude,* she's so *hot!*" As if I didn't know.)

I let the guys out through the front door and returned to the couch, where I had spent the entire morning. The television was still on and I sank back into position on the couch, flat on my back except for my head, which I propped up on a throw pillow. I picked up the remote and started flipping channels.

Saturday television is an abomination. The one day of the week when most people don't feel guilty about sitting in front of the boob tube and letting their brain melt for hours on end, and what do they put on? *Overboard,* that totally pointless, totally humorless 1980s Goldie Hawn flick that they've shown at least fourteen hundred times. I practically have the thing memorized from watching it throughout my childhood when there was nothing else on. My other choices were a *Law & Order* marathon, some reality TV crap where they show weddings from beginning to end, infomercials, cooking shows, and, of course, college football. Who the hell cares about college football, anyway? A bunch of talentless scrubs running around the field and doing fifteen-minute-long celebration dances after sacking a guy who didn't even *try* to get out of the way? It's like, get drafted, make a *real* team, then we'll talk.

My thumb was on autopilot. I was hitting the up button over and over and over again, as if scrolling through the channels for the fourth time was going to somehow change what was on. It was two o'clock in the afternoon and I had yet to change out of my pajamas—a Dave Matthews Band tour T-shirt, a pair of sweatpants, and my plaid flannel robe. (My dresser, being on the hallway side of my room, had miraculously survived. Thus I still had half my clothes and the box of practical joke paraphernalia I'd been hoarding since sleep-away camp, stuffed in the back of my underwear drawer.) My cereal bowl from that morning was on the floor next to me, along with a half-eaten box of doughnuts and four empty cans of Vanilla Coke. Considering my sugar intake for the day, I should have been running sprints around the living room, but just walking up the stairs with the guys had taken all the energy out of me. Somehow I felt like I couldn't move a single muscle in my body. Except, of course, for that thumb.

Oh, if Sarah could see me now. She was such a neat freak she'd almost fainted when she saw my bedroom. She'd spent half an hour organizing my CD collection while she decided which ones she wanted me to burn for her. It was so cute. Of course, the next day those CDs had been completely disorganized again. Maybe if I weren't such a slob, she wouldn't have broken up with me.

"Okay, that's it," I said to myself, tossing the remote on the glass-topped coffee table.

Aside from the squirrel in my closet, there wasn't another living thing in the house. Mom had left for work at the crack of dawn and the guys had only been here for two minutes. Other than that, I'd had no human contact.

I was acting pathetic, really. So Sarah had broken up with me. So she was dating some lame-o loser. So my room was a smoked-out haven for bushy-tailed rodents. So my father was in the hospital. So there was no conceivable way I was ever going to get my Jeep now. (A realization I'd come to in the middle of the night that had finally squeezed a couple of self-flagellating tears out of me.) That was no reason to sit around all day and feel sorry for myself. It was still Christmas, right? It was still, as the song goes, the most wonderful time of the year. And there was one thing that could always knock me out of any and all bad mood swings.

I pushed myself off the couch, prompting the head rush of the century, and staggered, half blind, over to the entertainment center. I braced my hands on top of the cabinet for a second and waited for the fog in my brain to clear, then dropped down and opened the deep drawer under the flat-screen TV. Inside were a couple of rows of videos that my parents had collected over the years. My mom's favorites: *Grease, Xanadu, Gone with the Wind, Mr. Mom.* My dad's favorites: *Beverly Hills Cop, Star Wars, Zulu.* (Don't ask.) Then, of course, there was our Christmas movie collection.

Everything from *Christmas Vacation* to *Miracle on 34th Street* (both the original and the newer one with that dude from *The Practice* and that woman from *Big*).

I slipped out the tape of *It's a Wonderful Life* and popped it into the VCR, causing the screen to go blue right in the middle of the minigolf montage of *Overboard.* Grabbing up the remote as I backed into the couch once again, I started to feel a little bit better. I was taking control. I was being proactive. I was not going to let outside forces get me down. And I was not going to let my mind wander back to our night at the movies again just because *I* was *watching* a movie. No. This was the new me.

I picked up my cell phone just to make sure Sarah hadn't called and the thing had neglected to ring (it happens!), then put it aside and hit the Play button on the remote.

I started to lie down again but stopped myself. No. I was going to sit up straight like a human being whose entire life had not been trashed less than twenty-four hours ago. I was going to watch my movie and cheer the hell up.

One hour later I was ready to put my bare foot through the television. *This* was supposed to be uplifting? What was wrong with Frank Capra, anyway? All poor Jimmy Stewart wanted to do was get out of his little nothing of a town and see the world! Why wouldn't they let him *do* it? Couldn't he just have gone on his little trip with his big monster trunk, come back, and *then* married Mary? And I have a hard time believing that a babe like Donna Reed ends up a lonely spinster librarian just because George Bailey doesn't exist. Come on! Were the rest of the guys in town born without *eyes* or something?

This movie was so contrived! It was so false! It was clearly made just to snow the viewing public into believing that their tiny little coupon-cutting, lawn-mowing lives were something more than they actually were so that they would keep going back to their dead-end jobs making money for big business and stuffing the bank accounts of the wealthy—the people who actually knew better.

And for God's sake, how the hell did Jimmy Stewart keep himself from strangling that annoying little Zuzu, anyway? I would've taken a shovel to her head somewhere in the middle of the first act.

I picked up the remote and flicked off the television in disgust. Maybe I would go to Blockbuster and rent *The Nightmare Before Christmas*. I'd always boycotted it on principle, but now I was kind of curious. Maybe Holly would let me borrow her copy.

Suddenly the front door opened and slammed and I sat up straight, startled. My eyes darted to the clock. It was only a little after three. My mother wasn't supposed to be home for a couple of hours. I was about to get up and go into the kitchen when I heard the distinct sound of my mother weeping and I stopped, my heart seizing up. Like I said, my mother rarely lost it, so when she did, it was kind of a scary thing. A scary thing I wasn't quite sure how to handle.

But my father, the one who knew exactly what to do in these situations, wasn't available. It was going to have to be me.

I stood up shakily, letting the fleece blanket I'd

wrapped around my legs fall to the ground, and tip-toed toward the kitchen, half hoping my mother would hear me and get ahold of herself. What was I supposed to do? I hated seeing my mother cry.

When I got to the kitchen, I hovered in the door-way for a moment. My mother had put a kettle of water on the stove and was pulling out the cocoa pow-der from above the microwave. She was wearing a knee-length skirt, a silk shirt, and heels, and she was all coiffed, just like she always was for work. Was there some problem with our insurance? Or was something wrong with Dad?

"Mom?" I said tentatively.

She dropped the measuring spoon into the cocoa can and turned around, wiping under her eyes with both hands.

"Paul! You startled me!" she said, faking a smile. Her eyes traveled down my body. "Are you still in your pajamas?"

Guilt settled over me like an iron blanket. "Yeah," I said. "Sorry. I just—"

"It's all right," she said, waving her hand and turn-ing back to her cocoa. "Maybe it's a good idea. I just might join you. . . ."

And then she started crying again, her shoulders shaking. I couldn't take it anymore.

"Mom? What's wrong?" I asked, walking into the kitchen and leaning into the back of one of the wooden chairs around the table.

"Ooooh . . . I was fired," my mother said. Actually, she almost sang it in her high-pitched voice. Like she was saying, "Ooooh . . . I'm so happeeeeeee!"

"What?" I blurted out. "Why?"

My mother shrugged as she measured out enough cocoa to warm a wagon train in the dead of winter on the plains. She shook her head as she talked, spooning powder into mugs. I wondered if she was expecting someone or if she actually had cracked. I had a sinking feeling it was the latter.

"That Awful Woman saw me taking your return without the receipt and instead of *asking* me what I was doing and maybe *waiting* for an explanation, she went directly to Mr. Steiger and told him she'd seen me taking an illegal return." She dropped her spoon and turned to me, her eyes wide and red. "She used the word 'illegal'! Like I'm some kind of common criminal!"

"I don't believe this," I said, my heart hardening into a heavy, cold stone. I pulled out the chair and dropped into it, resting my head in my hands. "That Awful Woman" was the euphemism my mother used for Marge Horvath, the assistant manager who had made me pry the pendant out of her bony little fingers the day before. Well, actually, made *Holly* pry it out of her fingers.

"Mr. Steiger called me into his office and told me that my conduct was unacceptable, and then he started telling me that there has been some money missing from registers recently and he was going to call a meeting about it tonight, anyway, but that since the money is always missing after my shifts, they were pretty certain that they had their culprit and this solidified it."

My mother was babbling now, her voice steadily rising in pitch until it could be heard only by mice and small dogs. All I could do was stare down at the holly-bordered place mats on the table and listen to the little voice in my head taunting me. *This is all your fault, all your fault, all your fault.* The voice sounded suspiciously like the elves from my prefire nightmare.

"They think I'm a thief, Paul! They think I've been stealing from them!"

Suddenly my mother seemed to realize that she had measured out half the can of cocoa and that there was nobody here to drink it. Her shoulders collapsed and she brought her hand to her head.

"It's gonna be okay, Mom," I said, even though I had no proof that this was in any way true.

"I'm sorry, sweetie," she said, sniffling. She sat down at the table right across from me and picked at the corner of the place mat in front of her, looking like a forlorn little girl. It's pretty weird when you see your mother so vulnerable. It kind of makes you feel like you aren't a kid anymore.

I got up, walked around behind her, and wrapped my arms around her back. She reached up and patted my forearms, then took a deep breath and let it out slowly.

"What would I do without you?" she said quietly.

Then I *really* didn't feel like a kid. I wanted to say something to make her feel better. Anything encouraging. But nothing came to mind. It seemed like the spirit of Scrooge had settled in over our once Christmas-spirited household and I had no idea how to make it go away.

For the first time in my life, Christmas Sucked with a capital *S*.

*   *   *

"Make it fast, man. We gotta get to the gym before the rush," Marcus told me as I jumped out of his car in front of the Foot Locker at Paramus Park on Monday afternoon.

"I'm gonna be two seconds," I told him, slamming the door.

I ran around the car and dodged a few shoppers to get to the automatic sliding door. The last place in the world I wanted to be at that moment was the mall—the proverbial scene of the crime—but I'd promised my mother I would pick up her last paycheck. There was no way she wanted to face That Awful Woman or Mr. Steiger again and I was glad I could do something for her. I just wanted to do it as quickly as humanly possible.

The mall was packed, as it would be every day until Christmas from here on out. I tried not to pay attention to the Muzak playing overhead or notice any of the bright decorations all around me. It had taken two days to entirely change the way I felt about this mall. Friday I'd been, let's face it, aglow. Today I was Mr. Sneer—the guy I hated. That person who stormed through the mall at Christmastime with that look on his face like it was a chore rather than a special yearly ritual to be savored and cherished.

I loathed myself.

I crossed the mall quickly, averting my eyes from the North Pole, and was about to duck right into Fortunoff and back to the counter in front of the office, but I stopped short, my sneakers squeaking on the linoleum. This was not happening. Sarah was not standing with Lainie Lefkowitz and That Awful Woman at the counter in the front of the store.

I stood there for a moment, unsure of how to proceed. Did I just walk by them, pretending they weren't even there as Sarah had done to me *all day long* in school? (I'd tried to talk to her during choir, but she'd told me she wasn't good with breakups and it would just be better if I left her alone right now. Please.) Did I act like the bigger person and just walk over there and say hello? Or did I, as the more sadistic part of my brain was prompting me to do, break open the emergency fire hose case next to me and douse all three of them with a nice, freezing-cold blast of water?

As I stood hovering, my decision was made for me by the none-too-subtle Lainie. She saw me standing there, elbowed Sarah on the arm, and lifted her chin in my direction. I quickly ran my hands through my hair and tucked in the front hem of my shirt. Sarah turned, paled, and swallowed.

"Uh . . . hi, Paul," she said.

"Oh, so I guess I'm not invisible outside of school," I said. Damn! Did I really *say* that? Way to act cool, buddy. I walked the few steps it took to join them and pointedly looked away from That Awful Woman. But from the corner of my eye I could see her with a wicked smirk on her pointy little face. Was she gloating over my booted mother or did she somehow, with her evil radar, know that I was a dumpee, standing next to my dumper?

"I heard about your house, Paul. I'm really sorry," Sarah said, her blue eyes sympathetic. Ugh! Why not just shoot a poisoned arrow through my heart? "Were you able to save any of your things?"

"Some of it. Thanks for asking," I said as I tried to

avoid That Awful Woman's amused gaze. "What are you buying?" I asked. There was a small silver Fortunoff box sitting on the counter in front of Sarah.

"Oh . . . well . . . Scooby gave me this present this afternoon and I was just bringing it back here to have it cleaned," Sarah said, her skin growing attractively pink. (Stop thinking that way!) "It was a little smudged. . . ."

Against my will, my brain was skipping around, jabbering about how pretty she was, how sweet she was to ask about my stuff, and how cute it was that she was embarrassed to be caught with another gift. That had to mean she cared about me, right? If she cared about the fire? If it mattered to her how I felt about another Scooby gift? It wasn't like she didn't think about me at—

My happy-thought train hit a brick wall when Sarah opened the little box and pulled out a delicate gold chain with a one-of-a-kind gold-and-ruby heart pendant dangling from the end.

"Isn't it gorgeous?" Lainie Lefkowitz gushed.

That was when I knew. Christmas wasn't just punishing me. It was out to destroy me. And it was enjoying the process.

I turned and faced the counter, looked Marge Horvath directly in her dirt-colored eyes, and said, "My mom's paycheck, please."

"I have it right here," she said, the smirk growing smirkier. She hit a few buttons on the register behind her and the drawer clanged open. She hadn't even fully turned around again before I'd snatched the envelope from between her claws and was halfway across the mall.

I was shocked at my ability to walk away. I really

thought that either my legs were going to go out from under me or my entire head was going to explode all over the Oriental Ornament cart. How was it possible that Scooby had bought the exact same necklace I'd chosen? There were about a million pieces of jewelry in that place. I mean, was he psychic? Was he some kind of sadistic mind-reading wanna-be rapper who'd been sent by Christmas to destroy me the moment I'd lost my Santa hat?

This time I wasn't going to avoid the North Pole. I wanted to look my enemy dead in the eye. I wanted to see if he had a nice big *666* painted across his forehead that I had somehow missed. But the closer I got to the Santa Shack and Scooby's velvet throne, the more my vision blurred. I had never felt such a surge of vindictive anger before in my life. I imagined myself morphed into a Godzilla-sized Paul, stalking through the center of the mall and crushing the Santa Shack, the whole North Pole, and Scooby underneath my massive feet.

There he sat with a couple of twin girls on his knees, bouncing them up and down and letting out a seriously lame excuse for a "ho ho ho." My hands clenched into fists, crushing the envelope that held my mother's paycheck. There was only one thought in my mind.

Santa must die.

I turned away from Scooby and all the fresh-faced, wide-eyed, clueless little kids. Soon, *very* soon, Scooby was going to feel my wrath. The wrath of a Christmas freak whom Christmas had forsaken.

Scooby was going down.

WHY AM I SUCH A MISFIT?
I AM NOT JUST A NITWIT!

ON TUESDAY AFTERNOON I FINALLY SAW WHAT SCOOBY looked like outside a Santa suit, and I was not impressed. He was training me, so he was dressed in one of the elf costumes—big green shoes with bells on the curled toes, red-and-white-striped tights, a green jumper thing, and a white turtleneck. His cheeks had red circles on them and he was wearing fake pointed ears and a floppy green-and-red elf hat. He looked like a joke, but in my personal opinion, he would have looked like a joke even in street clothes.

Scooby had a large nose, blond hair that I swear was prematurely thinning, a few patches of unimpressive stubble, skinny little lips, and a huge, *huge* Adam's apple. I mean, the thing was totally distracting. Every time he spoke to me, I found myself staring at it as it bobbed up and down, up and down, like a tetherball on its string.

What in the name of good Saint Nick did Sarah *see* in this guy?

"Hey, loser, you're doing it wrong," Scooby said to me through his tight fake smile. He was standing next to the Santa throne, where I sat under ten pounds of padding, waiting for the next overweight kid to climb onto my lap. I'm telling you, nine out of ten of these kids should have been asking for exercise videos and subscriptions to Weight Watchers.

"Doing *what* wrong?" I asked, the synthetic fibers of my beard sticking to my lips.

"You're sitting all wrong," Scooby said.

I felt my body heat rise, which seemed impossible considering the buckets I was already sweating in the heavy wool suit. Trying to smile at the little pigtailed girl who was tentatively approaching, I decided to bite my tongue, which wasn't easy. Since I'd donned the Santa suit a few hours earlier, Scooby had managed to criticize my laugh, my belly, my posture, my walk, the twinkle in my freakin' eyes, and now the way I was *sitting*?

"And what's your name?" I asked the little girl, who was now rocking back and forth in front of me, her tiny hands clasped behind her back and her lips pressed together so tightly they'd disappeared.

"Tameeka!" she blurted out.

"Well, come on up here, Tameeka," I said in my best Santa voice.

I held out my arms to her and that seemed to be all she needed to come right out of her shell. She hurled her entire body at me, flinging her arms onto my chest and sort of dangling there between my legs. Trying not to groan, I adjusted her until she was sitting on my knee, grateful for the extra padding the suit had in the groin area. If it hadn't been there, little Tameeka would have heard a stream of highly inappropriate expletives.

"I want a karaoke machine!" Tameeka announced, clapping. "And I want it to have all of Aaliyah's songs, even though she died, and all of Britney Spears's songs and all of Janet Jackson's songs—"

"Ho ho ho!" I chuckled. "You sure know a lot about music."

"My older brother Joaquin is a DJ!" Tameeka announced proudly. "He says I'm gonna be a star!"

"A DJ! *Real*-ly?" Scooby said, breaking the cardinal rule of elfdom—no talking to the kids unless they need to be pried away. Apparently most tiny tots were even more afraid of the elves than they were of Santa. "Is this brother of yours here?"

I was about to tell Scooby to back off when Tameeka turned around and gave him a look that could only be called sassy. "And who the hell are *you*?" she asked.

Scooby blanched and stood up straight and I had to stifle a laugh. "A karaoke machine," I said to Tameeka. "Have you been a good girl?"

"You better believe it!" Tameeka said. "I do all my chores *and* my brother's *and* I gave half my books to the needy this year. I didn't want to, but my mom made me and I think that should count for something."

"Ho ho ho," I said. I liked this girl. "You're quite right, Tameeka. I'll see what I can do about that karaoke machine. Have a merry Christmas, now!"

"Thanks, Santa!" Tameeka said. She slid off my lap

and gave Scooby one last scathing look before running off to her waiting parents.

"Why did you let her go?" Scooby demanded.

"What? She didn't have a card," I replied. If a kid's parents pay for a picture with Santa, the kid is given a little card and that means Santa has to hold on to him or her and pose for the photographer elf, a depressed photography student named Quentin, who was dressed up as a reindeer.

"Forget the card, loser! You totally forgot to mention my CD," Scooby said. "She was a prime target."

"They're not targets, *Scooby*, they're kids," I told him through my teeth.

"Well, la-di-freakin'-da!" Scooby said, bending back and waving his hands in the air. "Look at Mr. High and Mighty! Guess your Goody Two-shoes attitude didn't get you very far with Sarah."

I tried really, really hard to keep the angry flush from rising to my face, but there was nothing I could do. And the second Scooby saw it, he knew he had me. And once he knew he had me, it was all over.

"Aw! Did I hit a *sore* spot?" he taunted me. "You miss your little girlfriend, do ya? I guess I can see why. She *is* the best kisser I've ever had in my life and I've had plenty, if ya know what I mean. . . ."

Scooby had definitely mastered the single entendre.

I stared at the line of children and their parents in front of me, willing the little boy who was bawling and clinging to his mother to just get a grip and get the heck over here. He was holding up the line and if I didn't have a kid on my lap soon, Scooby was going to keep going and eventually I was going to have to rip his head off. And I really didn't think the management of Paramus Park was going to look too kindly on a Santa who traumatized his patrons with a bloody Christmas massacre.

"And that lip gloss she wears, *man*!" He inhaled slowly and closed his eyes in bliss as if he were smelling that strawberry goodness right then and there. "It tastes *so* good. . . ."

My hands clenched into big red fists on the armrests of the throne. I was going to overheat. I was going to melt out of my skin. My back stuck to the T-shirt I wore under my costume and every inch of my body was bathed in sweat. My eyes stung as I glared down at the screaming little boy and all the other kids grasping their mothers' hands, jabbering on about what they wanted, what they *had* to have. Overhead, "White Christmas" poured from the crackling speakers for the fifth time that hour, raising all the hairs on the back of my neck with its unabashed optimism. What was Bing Crosby crooning about? This holiday was a joke. The decorations were garish and offensive, the kids were all greedy little monkeys, the guys in the Santa suits were pathetic teenagers who were trying to sell CDs to an unsuspecting public and fighting over girls!

". . . and I don't think it's gonna be long before she gives it *all* up, if ya know what I mean—"

That was it. I snapped. I started to push myself away from the Santa throne and was about to turn and grab Scooby right by that Adam's apple when—

"Okay, Paul, your shift's over."

I blinked. There, standing in front of me, was Eve Elias, the elf who had been working the line, her golden blond hair tied into two long braids. I cooled off the instant I saw her. Little did she know she'd just saved us all from appearing on the six o'clock news.

"I already put up the sign, so you can go in the shack and change," she said, gesturing behind her at the red ropes and the little wooden sign that read, Santa Will Be Back in Fifteen Minutes. The screaming kid had calmed down now that his impending doom had been postponed.

"Thanks," I said, shakily pushing myself out of the chair and trudging over to the Santa Shack. The second the door was closed, I yanked off the beard and hat and felt the cool mall air chill my wet scalp. I peeled off the suit and sure enough, my T-shirt and boxers clung to me. When I pulled the fabric away, the air rushed over my skin, chilling out my temper as well as my body.

Okay. Everything was going to be okay.

The door banged open and Scooby came in. He looked me up and down and let out a cackle.

"Been swimming?" he asked, popping open his locker and grabbing his Santa suit. I turned my back to him and hustled into my jeans and sneakers, then grabbed my sweater and bailed. The last thing I needed to see was a half-naked Scooby.

Holly was supposed to be picking me up in fifteen minutes, but I couldn't wait. I went to grab my cell phone to see if she was on her way and stopped. Tipping back my head, I let out a strangled moan. My jacket. I'd left my jacket in the Santa Shack.

I stalked back to the North Pole and up to the shack, where I yanked open the back door. Nothing could have prepared me for what I saw inside—Scooby, in all his scrawny paleness, flexing nonexistent muscles in front of the mirror, wearing a pair of black boxers with the words *Love Machine* printed across the butt in red glitter.

Much to my surprise, Scooby didn't even flinch when he saw me standing there. He didn't blush. He didn't grab his clothing. He simply turned, did a bodybuilder tricep flex (again, nothing to flex), and looked up at me.

"You all right, loser?" he asked. "Now that you know what your girl is gettin'?"

I reached over to the chair in the corner, picked up my jacket, and left without a word. Scooby was, without a doubt, the biggest dork I'd ever come across in all my seventeen years. And somehow, for some reason, Sarah had chosen this sorry excuse for a human over me. Part of me knew I should just write them off right then and there. Scooby was obviously pathetic and Sarah must be harboring some kind of weird dork fetish.

But no. That wasn't possible. Sarah was amazing. She was perfect. She loved my Jeep obsession and wore my sweater to bed and smelled like peppermint and didn't mind publicly cuddling at the movies. This wasn't the type of girl who wasted her time on dorks. Scooby had brainwashed her somehow. She never would have hooked up with him otherwise. She clearly had no idea what she'd gotten herself into. And the idea that Scooby was pulling one over on the love of my life only made me hate him more. I couldn't let him get away with it. But the question was, what was I going to do now?

*   *   *

"You look like death," Holly said when I got into her car.

"Thanks," I replied, balling my jacket and sweater up in my lap. I popped the seat back until I was horizontal and closed my eyes.

"What happened to you in there?" Holly asked as she peeled out.

"I can't believe I'm about to say this, and to you of all people, but I think I hate Christmas."

Holly hit the brakes and my eyes flew open, my hands flinging out instinctively to brace myself for the impending crash. But when I sat up, there was nothing. No cars. No pedestrians. Slowly I looked up at Holly. She had a look of maniacal glee on her face not unlike the one the Grinch sports after he comes up with the idea to steal Christmas from the Whos.

Slamming on the gas again, Holly swung into a handicapped spot and put the car in park. "Are you serious, or are you just experiencing a momentary lapse of Paulness?" she asked as she twisted herself around and started digging for something in her canvas bag in the backseat.

"Oh, I'm serious," I told her. "You know what's been going through my head all day? Three words: *Santa must die.* I swear, Holly, I really think I'm losing touch here."

"You're not losing touch, you're just . . . seeing things in a new light," Holly said, flopping down in her seat again, now clutching a piece of wrinkled paper. "In the real light of day," she added. She handed over the paper and watched me expectantly.

It wasn't without reservations that I unfolded the page to read its contents. Holly was acting hyper and weird, even for her. But I have to admit, I was curious.

"The Anti-Christmas Underground?" I read from across the top of the page. The letters were big and black and two Santa feet were sticking out from under the *d* as if he'd been flattened like the Wicked Witch of the West. "Where did you get this?" I asked.

"From Rudy Snow," Holly said, biting her bottom lip in excitement. "Look! They have weekly meetings, but I've never gotten up the guts to go. Now you can go with me!"

"Wait a second, wait a second," I said. "Rudy Snow? The new kid with the obvious hyperactivity disorder?" This guy started school with us at the beginning of the year and proceeded to earn a rep for singing out loud during exams, shouting out answers before the teacher was finished asking them, and spontaneously break dancing in the cafeteria. Of course, he did always have a smile on his face, so maybe he actually knew something the rest of us didn't.

"He's really nice," Holly told me. "Look, he came up to me after history because he saw me doodling a Christmas tree with a big *X* over it, and that's when he gave me this flyer. He and his friends have this Web site, Ihatechristmas.com. I checked it out during computer tech and it was totally cool."

I looked at Holly's elated expression and realized, for the first time, exactly how deep her distaste for Christmas actually ran. I mean, I always knew she hated the season—that every year she just couldn't wait to get December over with and move on. But here she was, willing to join a militant anti-Christmas organization. The girl was *serious*. Maybe even obsessed.

"The Anti-Christmas Underground?" I repeated, scanning the page. Aside from a meeting time and place, the notice said that only Santa haters need apply. Across the bottom was what I assumed was the group's motto: Dedicated to Truth, Justice, and the Eradication of the Christmas Spirit.

"What do you think?" Holly asked.

What did I think? I wasn't sure if my brain was even functioning properly. But there was a strange sort of tingly feeling rushing up my spine. An almost tangible sense of euphoria. I started to sit up straight, my mouth nearly watering, the fog in my brain lifting. This was it. This was what I needed to fight back against the holiday that had declared all-out war on me and my family. I needed a coalition. An army. Compadres. Mates. Comrades in arms. I needed the Anti-Christmas Underground. I looked at Holly and her whole face lit up before I even said the words.

"Let's do it."

It was already dark out when Holly and I approached the back door of a small redbrick house in Fair Lawn, our breath making steam clouds in the cold. The directions Rudy had given Holly instructed us to go down the outdoor basement steps, knock, and wait. I have to admit, I was a little freaked out. Strange neighborhood, strange directions, going to see a bunch of potential psychos I didn't even know. I had the chills even without the subzero temperature. But I also felt a bit like James Bond on a mission. Which was fairly cool.

Holly knocked and a few paint chips scattered from the wooden door, which looked like it had been shedding color for years. We waited. And waited. And the longer we stood there, the more the hairs on the back of my neck stood on end. There was something not quite right about all this.

"Maybe we should just—"

The door opened with a painful creak. A huge kid about our age with Asian features and dyed blond hair opened the door just wide enough to sandwich his large belly and make it protrude even more. He looked at us through thick glasses, his expression sullen and suspicious at the same time. His black T-shirt read, Give Me a Dollar and I'll Leave You Alone.

"How did you find us?" he asked flatly.

"Rudy Snow invited me," Holly replied, stuffing her mittened hands under her arms and shuffling her feet against the cold.

"Dirk!" the kid shouted, startling us both. I actually jumped. "We got newbies!"

"Hold on!" a muffled voice called out from the basement depths.

The big kid produced a sandwich the size of my head from behind his back and took a bite, chewing as he stared at us blankly. My eyes met Holly's.

"Okay! Bring 'em in!" the same muffled voice shouted.

The big kid turned around and left the door ajar, saying nothing. Holly and I hesitated a moment before following.

Our greeter led us through a small, dank, cinder-block-walled space that reeked of mildew and wet paper into a huge room. It ran the length of the house and was lit by dimmed fluorescent torchlights in each corner. The wood-paneled walls were decorated with posters from Christmas movies, each of which had been defaced in some sadistic way. Tim Allen's eyes were gouged out on the poster from *The Santa Clause* and Macaulay Culkin had been drawn to look like the devil on the *Home Alone* poster. But the *Emmet Otter's Jug-Band Christmas* poster—which is very rare, by the way—was the worst. All the little swampland animals were holding machine guns and machetes that must have been cut out of *Guns & Ammo* and pasted on. Their faces were sketched over with markers to wear looks of battle-ready rage, and Emmet himself was sporting a gas mask.

I turned in circles as I followed our guide across the room, taking in broken Christmas decorations, a beheaded Rudolph doll, stacks of videotapes marked with the names of Christmas specials from the last ten years. Wondering what purpose these served, I walked backward into something heavy and semisoft that felt like a person. In the midst of cardiac arrest, I whirled around and grabbed on to a large swinging punching bag that hung from one of the ceiling beams. On it was a poorly painted replica of Santa Claus; his face had been so pummeled it was barely there anymore.

"You okay?" Holly asked over the roaring of blood in my ears.

"Not quite sure," I replied.

A loud sizzle and crackle caught our attention and we both flinched. Sitting in the far corner of the room was a police scanner, belching out codes and car numbers. Above it was a large relief map of Bergen and Rockland counties with pins stuck into various spots and huge red arrows pointing at others. I swallowed hard. I wasn't sure whether to be repulsed or intrigued.

"Dirk, newbies. Newbies, Dirk," the big kid said, his mouth full. We stopped at the edge of a wooden coffee table that was surrounded by three couches in various stages of decay. The big kid sat down next to a girl half his size on the couch to our right. Across from them Rudy was perched on the edge of his seat, fidgeting as always. He grinned and raised his eyebrows at us.

Dirk, a small guy wearing cargo pants and a wife beater, stood up from the couch across from us. He was clearly the leader. He had a presence. And although he was small, he was definitely a free-weights kind of person. He had defined arms and held them away from his sides like a chronic bodybuilder.

"Welcome to the Anti-Christmas Underground," Dirk said. Then his face suddenly contorted and, one eye winking closed, his whole head jerked to the right. I blinked, but no one else seemed to notice, so I pretended I didn't, either. Holly took an almost imperceptible step closer to me. I somehow resisted the urge to grab her hand and run.

"I'm Dirk, and this . . . is my place," he said, opening his arms wide. "I got this twitch when I was five years old. I was kicked in the nuts by a rabid reindeer at a petting zoo. Had it ever since."

I held back the nervous laugh that pushed its way up my throat.

"This here's Flora. She goes to Northern Valley," he said, gesturing to the girl on the couch. She had short dark hair, pale skin, and red-rimmed glasses and was dressed in head-to-toe black. "Flora hasn't believed in Santa Claus since she was two years old. That's the year she started getting underwear and socks under the tree."

"Nothing but underwear and socks," Flora said in a quiet, sweet, dreamy-sounding voice that made me suspect she was heavily drugged. "Every year." She looked down at the closed notebook on her lap.

"You've already met Ralph, our Paramus Catholic man," Dirk continued, with another wink and a twitch. "He once had a department store Santa call him 'lardass' in front of a hundred waiting kids and their parents."

"They still laugh in my nightmares," Ralph said before ripping another hunk off his sandwich with his teeth.

"And you know Rudy. He's originally from Fair Lawn like me," Dirk said, turning to the other couch.

"Hey! How ya doin'? I'm Rudy! Nice to meet ya!" he said, looking at me. Sporting a Yankees jersey, a flat-top, and some peach fuzz over his lip, Rudy stood up and shook my hand over the table. He had a serious grip. "Last Christmas my mom and I had to move in with my great-aunt Rita. Rita has a three-room apartment and she sucks her teeth and makes me rub her corns and I think maybe she has something rotting in her bedroom closet because the smell from in there is, like, bottom-of-the-garbage-pail rank, but I haven't been able to get past her to find out what it is."

With that, Rudy smiled and sat down, his left leg jiggling like it wanted to free itself from the rest of his body. He continued to watch us with that eager smile.

"So, you've met us," Dirk said, turning his palms up in a gesture that made me think of *The Godfather*. "Now we just have two questions for you and then we'll take a vote and consider you for membership."

Holly and I exchanged a look. There was no turning back now.

"You," Dirk said, lifting his chin at Holly and looking her over in a manner that inexplicably made me want to punch him in the face. "What's your name?"

"I'm Holly," she replied, touching her hand to her chest.

"Holly. Funny. As in 'deck the halls with'?" Dirk said, snorting a laugh that prompted the others to titter and shift in their seats. "Okay, *Holly*. What did Christmas do to you?" Dirk asked. He folded his hands together at zipper level—a pose that accentuated his triceps—and waited with a skeptical expression.

"Two years ago my dad left us on Christmas morning for a department store elf," Holly said matter-of-factly. "Haven't heard from him since."

You could hear the intake of breath in the room. The three kids on the couches looked up at Dirk, but his face remained impassive—then twitched violently.

"And you are?" he asked, turning his cleft chin toward me.

"Paul," I replied. My voice, to my horror, sounded like Peter Brady's in the "Time to Change" episode. I cleared my throat.

"Paul, what did Christmas do to you?" Dirk asked.

"Well, let's see," I said, shifting my weight from one foot to the other. "On the day after Thanksgiving, I bought the love of my life a necklace I couldn't afford and she subsequently dumped my butt for the Paramus Park Santa, a loser named Scooby who has a rap fetish and a really big Adam's apple. And when my mother returned said necklace at her store, she got fired for not having a receipt. Oh, and the *reason* she didn't have the receipt was because my father started a fire at my house after being electrocuted while hanging Christmas lights and the fire gutted my room and destroyed pretty much everything, including the receipt. Now my dad's in the hospital, my mother's depressed, my ex isn't talking to me, and I'm not getting the Jeep I was promised for Christmas because the repairs on the house and the hospital bills are costing too much. And oh yeah, I spent all *my* money on a suit and a tie and a ticket for a dance that I'm no longer going to, so to top it all off, I'm broke."

I paused for breath and Rudy let out an impressed whistle. Everyone in the room looked at Dirk, who couldn't take his eyes off me. There was this glint there that I couldn't quite identify, but it kind of felt like admiration. A smile pulled at the corners of my mouth.

"We don't have to vote," Dirk said finally, his words punctuated by another violent twitch. "You two are in."

WE'LL FROLIC AND PLAY
THE ESKIMO WAY . . .

THE NEXT DAY I WAS ON ELF DUTY. TECHNICALLY I WAS still in training, so I was supposed to observe Scooby at work all afternoon. Just thinking about it would have been torture, if not for the fact that I showed up for my shift armed with a lengthy list of creative ways to sabotage and humiliate Scooby. Thanks to the Anti-Christmas Underground, I had a whole new outlook on life. Dirk and his friends were weird, but Holly and I decided to join their club, anyway. After all, we were weird, too, and in the exact same way. Where else were you gonna find a bunch of kids who hated Christmas enough to form a coalition? Now I was going to strike back at the holiday with the Underground's help, and Scooby was going to be my first victim of war.

I walked out of the Santa Shack in my elf gear, feet jingling, and shoved my plan of attack into the little pocket on the front of the green jumper. Holly, Dirk, and Ralph stood at the foot of the snowy slope that surrounded the shack. They burst out laughing the moment they saw me. Dirk's head started to twitch uncontrollably. Apparently laughter made the problem even worse.

"Nice, you guys. Thanks a lot," I said as I approached them. But I was smiling. Nothing was going to get me down that day. I had the sweet taste of impending revenge on my tongue.

"This is a nice look for you," Holly said, putting her hand on my shoulder. "Is that from Keebler's fall line?"

"Good one, Hol," I said flatly. "Now, can we get to work, please?"

Dirk pushed up the sleeves of his fraying gray T-shirt and twitched. "Ralph's mom is already in line with the runt brigade. Follow me."

Holly, Ralph, and I did as instructed. We came around the Santa Shack to find a line of about thirty kids and their families snaking along the North Pole area and out toward Abercrombie & Fitch. Scooby was busy trying to convince the five-year-old on his lap that his rap album was better than Elmo's latest. I almost laughed at the unsuspecting schmuck. He had no idea what was coming.

"There they are—at two o'clock," Dirk said, lifting his chin.

I followed his gaze and saw a tiny, harried-looking Asian woman. A pair of huge kids, one boy and one girl, hung from her arms while another boy ran around her legs. The kids couldn't have been more than five years old, but together they definitely out-weighed their mother. As the line moved forward, she nudged a stroller, complete with a struggling toddler, along with her knee.

"*That's* your mom?" Holly asked, looking up at Ralph. He nodded.

"His dad's a *big* man," Dirk said under his breath.

Ralph nodded again.

"Yo, Ralph. Who's the runner?" Dirk asked, lifting his chin toward Ralph's family again.

"Cousin Doogie," Ralph said.

"Doogie?" I asked.

"My aunt liked that show," Ralph replied.

"Well, let's do this," Dirk said. He slapped my shoulder. Hard.

I nodded and stood up straight, rolling my shoulders back. As Dirk and I walked around the North Pole toward the line, my feet jingle jangled every step of the way. I could hear Holly and Ralph trailing behind me, snorting and giggling. I'm sure my soccer player's calves looked pretty comical in the striped tights. I heard a sudden "oof" and knew someone had just walked into Holly.

"Hey, Mrs. Ho. How ya doin'?" Dirk asked, approaching Ralph's mom.

She looked up at us, her eyes heavy. "Hello, Dirk," she said, attempting a smile. She saw Ralph standing behind us and registered surprise. "I thought you told me you'd only enter the mall at Christmastime over your own dead body."

I glanced at Ralph, but he just stared back at his mom impassively. I couldn't imagine him uttering the number of words his mother had just attributed to him.

"Mrs. Ho, this is Paul and that's Holly," Dirk said. She nodded at each of us. "Ralph thought we should offer to wait with the kids for you—you know, give you a little time off your feet."

More surprise. In fact, Mrs. Ho looked like she was about to cry. "Really?" she said. "That would be wonderful." She shook off the two kids and walked around Dirk, straightening her coat and sweater. "Sometimes you really are the sweetest boy," she said, reaching up to grab Ralph's flushed cheeks. She pulled him down and laid a big, smacking kiss on his forehead, then scurried away so fast she left a Mrs. Ho–sized blur behind her.

"Gotta love Mrs. Ho," Dirk said. He nodded to Ralph and Holly, who reached into their backpacks. Then Dirk shoved his hands in his pockets and looked down at the kids. "Hey, Roger . . . Mandy. 'Member me?"

Roger and Mandy looked up at me and Dirk with trepidation, their chubby cheeks splotched with pink. Doogie took a couple of steps back as if he was getting ready to bolt.

"Hey, kids," I said, kneeling down to their level. "Going to see Santa, huh?"

Mandy started pulling in staggering gasps of air, a clear precursor to a loud wail. What was wrong with me? It was like I'd spaced on the whole elf-fear thing. I was about to panic when Holly and Ralph provided us with the key element to the plan—eight twenty-ounce bottles of soda.

"Want something to drink, guys?" Holly asked with her best baby-sitter's smile. She might be invisible to adults, but Holly prided herself on her kid magnetism. She was the most sought-after baby-sitter in town.

"Soda!" little Mandy cried out, reaching up her arms and bouncing up and down. Dirk and Holly twisted open the bottles and handed one to each ambulatory kid.

"What about Davy?" Ralph asked.

"Want soda! Want soda!" the baby shouted, reaching out his arms as he continued to squirm.

"You can't give a toddler soda," Holly told Ralph. "He'll be bouncing off the walls."

"But he wants one," Ralph said in his usual monotone.

Holly laughed. "You can't just give them everything they want," she said.

Ralph shrugged and knelt down in front of the stroller, trying to distract the now screeching toddler.

As the line inched along, the children sucked down sodas as if they were going out of style. You'd think no one had ever let these kids drink anything with sugar in it before. But it was all good. Perfect, actually. We wanted to get as much liquid into them as possible before they got to Scooby's lap.

I glared at Scooby as the line moved forward. He was so smug, sitting up there in his Santa suit, his Adam's apple practically visible under the thick beard. (I swear I could see the fake hair bobbing up and down in that area.) Thought he could steal my girlfriend and get away with it, did he? Well, he had another think coming.

"We're next," Holly whispered to me, sending a thrill of anticipation down my spine.

I could just imagine the look on Scooby's face when he was covered in kiddie pee. I wondered which of my new little friends would be the one to get him. Roger was starting to jump up and down, but Mandy appeared to be the front-runner. She had her knees clamped together and her face was turning a bright pink to match her Powerpuff Girls sneakers.

"Paulie! We have a situation here," Dirk said under his breath.

I glanced up. Melissa Maya, the assistant mall manager (say that ten times fast), was whispering something in Scooby's ear. They both scanned the area and when their eyes fell on me, Melissa snapped her fingers frantically and waved me over. My friends and I were standing right at the head of the line and now Doogie, too, was starting to squirm.

"I'll be right back," I told them, walking up the velvet carpet.

Melissa barely looked at me. "Peter, we need your help."

"It's Paul," I said.

"Like I care," she replied. "Mr. Papadopoulos wants to talk to Scooby and he wants to talk to him now, so you gotta get in costume and take the throne."

My face must have gone white. "Now?" I asked.

"We just had a Santa break. We take another one and the little freaks'll go berserk." Melissa eyed the children in line. "Buncha little chunk munchers."

Clearly she wasn't a kid person.

"But what if they recognize—"

"Look, Percy," Melissa said, suddenly turning on me with dilated pupils that I swear flashed red for a split second. She had little lines around her eyes that looked like pitchforks. "Either you get your butt in that shack right now or I'll fire it. If I have to stay down here one second longer with these money-wasting freaks, I'm going to explode and I'm going to take you with me."

Clearly not a mall person, either. Kinda makes you wonder how she ended up here.

I glanced helplessly back at my friends, now surrounded by four dancing, squirming children, and walked into the Santa Shack. I changed my clothes slowly, trying to think of a way out, but when I glanced out the window, Melissa Maya was standing there waiting for me and Scooby was on his way upstairs. There was nothing I could do. I was going to have to play Santa for four full-bladdered kids.

"All set," I said, emerging from the shack moments later.

"Okay!" Melissa shouted. "Santa's back! Next child, please!"

Holly, Dirk, and Ralph didn't move. Holly was looking at me, her eyes wide, willing me to tell her what to do. I held my breath and shrugged. With one of my bosses standing right there, we were trapped.

"Santa's waiting!" Melissa said impatiently. Ralph, who was busy downing the last of the bottles of soda, nearly spat it all out.

Holly scurried forward with Mandy and deposited her on my lap.

"I have to go to the bafoom," Mandy said, squirming.

"Ho ho ho," I said quickly. "Okay, then, what do you want for Christmas?"

"My own 'puter," Mandy said. She clamped her hands between her legs.

"Get her out of there!" Dirk mouthed down at the end of the carpet.

"Okay, your own computer, you got it," I told Mandy. "Merry Christmas!"

Holly hustled Mandy away and Ralph walked up to me, holding Roger up against his massive chest. He sat him down on my legs without a word, raised his eyebrows in a what-can-I-do gesture, and turned away.

"Ho ho ho," I said. "What do you want for Christmas?"

Roger burst into tears. "I want my mom! I want my *mom*!" he screeched.

"I need some Advil," Melissa Maya said. She turned and stalked away, holding a hand to her forehead.

I got Roger off my lap and waved frantically at Dirk to bring me Davy. The kid sat there calmly and stared at my beard, then toddled off. I breathed a sigh of relief. The danger was over. Dirk walked up to me, deposited Doogie on my lap, and squeezed my shoulder.

"You made it," he said.

That was when Cousin Doogie relieved his tiny yet oddly high-capacity bladder all over my leg.

"Just go inside, take a shower, and you'll feel much better," Holly told me as she pulled the car to a stop in front of my house. She turned away, hiding her mouth with her hand.

"You can laugh," I told her. "It's not like I don't see the humor."

"I'm sorry," she said through uncontrollable giggles. "I'm really sorry, I just . . . I can't stop thinking about your face!"

Her laughter made me smile. I couldn't help it.

"See? Everything's going to be fine!" Holly said, finally managing to contain herself. "Ooh! I have an idea!" She brought her gloved hand down on my knee. (I'd washed off in the mall employee bathroom and changed back into my jeans.) "I'm sitting for the Hurleys tomorrow. Why don't I bring them to see Santa?"

"Oh, I love your brain!" I said, my face lighting up. "They'll crucify Scooby."

The Hurleys are the most infamous group of pre-pubescent delinquents around. The oldest one was caught stealing cigarettes at the ripe age of eight, and the youngest had been written up in the papers last year for punching the Thirty-fourth Street Macy's Santa in the face and breaking the guy's nose. Scooby would be powerless against their inherent wickedness.

"Holly, you are the best," I told her.

"Just wait until tomorrow night," she said. "The Underground is getting together to steal all the Santa displays from Midland Park to Montvale. Sounds like it's gonna be fun."

"I'm there," I told her. "See you tomorrow!"

I climbed out of the car and jogged up to the house, trying not to look up at my hole of a bedroom. All I wanted to do was take that shower, put on my pajamas, and crawl into the pullout bed in the den. Maybe I could get my mom to bring me my dinner in there and I wouldn't have to move for the rest of the night. I still couldn't believe my first Scooby plan had crashed and burned, but all would be well. With Holly and the others on my side, there was no way I could lose.

"Hey, Mom," I said, walking right by the kitchen.

I was halfway down the hall when I heard her call out my name, in a tone that suggested she thought I might have lost my mind.

"What's up?" I asked, turning to find her standing just outside the kitchen door. She had one hand on the doorjamb and one hand flat against her apron on her thigh. Her expression was concerned.

"What?" I asked.

"I'm . . . making fudge," she said, her eyebrows coming together.

"And?" I asked. Suddenly I could smell it. In fact, the smell had filled the house like it always did. It seemed to be coming out of the wallpaper. I was surprised I hadn't noticed it the second I walked in.

"When was the last time you walked by the kitchen when I was making fudge?" my mother asked.

"Probably never," I said, wanting this conversation to be over. I was suddenly very tired. Not even Christmas fudge appealed to me.

"Well, when I visited your father this afternoon, he mentioned he'd like us to bring him some. And I'm also making the gift packages for the family," my mother said, wiping both hands on her apron.

A stab of guilt hit my chest. I was going to go over to the hospital after work, but after the peeing incident, I hadn't been able to think of anything other than taking a long shower. Now visiting hours were over and I wouldn't get to see my dad until tomorrow. Could this day get any worse?

"Do you want to help?" my mother asked.

"Not tonight, Mom," I said. "I'm sorry, I'm just really tired from work."

"Well, speaking of work, it looks like I won't be completely unemployed for the holidays," she said. "Vivian's going to let me pick up some shifts."

"Vivian Black?" I asked, my stomach turning. "Mom, you don't mean—"

"Paul, it's not that bad," my mother said, turning to stir the fudge on the stove top.

Not that bad! I thought. Vivian Black ran the Hickory Farms kiosk and made all her employees wear head-to-toe reindeer outfits, complete with antlers and red pom-pom noses. Not only that, but the kiosk was right across from Fortunoff. All of my mom's old coworkers were going to be watching her hand out sausage samples in that humiliating outfit. I could just imagine the look on That Awful Woman's face.

"This is all my fault," I said, closing my eyes.

"Paul, none of this is your fault," my mother replied. "And it's just for December. In the new year I'll find something else." She turned around and flashed me her ever-bright smile. "Everything's going to be just fine. You'll see."

Part of my brain snapped at her to wake up and smell the coffee. Everything was *not* going to be fine! But I didn't say it. My mom hadn't *done* anything to me, after all. So why did I feel so angry all of a sudden?

"Okay," I said. "I'm gonna go do my homework."

As I headed for the bathroom, I realized it wasn't just anger. On top of the anger there was guilt. Whatever my mom said, it *was* my fault. She never would have been fired if she hadn't tried to return that necklace for me. And on top of the guilt was something else. I couldn't help feeling . . . sorry for my mother. I mean, how could she still be into all that cheery Christmas crap after everything that had happened? Making gift packages for the family? She'd been falsely accused of stealing and then fired! She'd gone from selling diamonds to hawking cheese! And now she was in there humming carols. How naive could she be? Christmas had turned on us. There was nothing to be merry about anymore.

I walked into the bathroom and turned on the hot water, stripping off my clothes. As soon as I had sloughed off about ten layers of my skin, I was going back to work on Project Scooby. Tomorrow I would have my revenge.

Do They Know It's
Christmastime at All?

"ALL RIGHT, EVERYONE, GOOD JOB," MR. MCDANIEL called out as he closed the *Les Misérables* music we'd been working on. "Let's turn to the carols."

"Don't faint on us now, Rudolph," Turk Martin said under his breath, leaning half an inch toward me. His smaller, more hyper sidekick, Randy Cook, cracked up laughing as I felt my face start to redden.

Both Randy and Turk totally got off on picking on me at Christmastime every year, trying to get me all riled up so that I would start spouting my "Most Wonderful Time of the Year" arguments. Little did they know that I was over it. Big-time. And I wasn't going to take their crap anymore.

"Shut up, Turk," I said.

Randy stopped laughing abruptly as some serious tension filled the air.

Turk turned toward me and gave me this confused look, as if my telling him to shut up was so absurd he couldn't quite process it. Of course, I understand why it would be difficult for him. No mere mortal has even looked him directly in the eye since the third grade. (That was the year he started shaving.) Turk Martin is one of those square-jawed angry kids who always has this perpetual squinty-eyed look like he's deciding whose butt to kick next.

I stood there, trying not to notice how much bigger he was than me and waiting for him to hit me with a right hook, but then McDaniel started the intro to "Deck the Halls" and I was saved by the music.

I sang my part with about one-tenth of the enthusiasm I usually had while singing carols. Usually at this time of year I wanted choir to last all day. Today I couldn't stop looking at the clock and wishing the second hand would hurry it up already. The moment the song was over, Turk turned to me again.

"Dude, what the hell is wrong with you? You're all off-key," he said as Mr. McDaniel turned his attention to the sopranos. He started going over their part of "Deck the Halls" with them, as if they needed any help. The sopranos were the ones who always got to sing the melody line of every song—the one we've all been hearing our entire lives. It's the rest of us who were stuck learning sucky harmonies for these sucky carols.

"Maybe I'm all fa-la-la-ed out, okay?" I snapped back.

Whoa. Did I just say that?

"Dude, what happened to Mr. Christmas?" Randy said, sounding almost disappointed. I guess he was wondering what he'd do to pass the time now that he had no reason to think up lame yuletide jokes.

When I didn't respond, Turk and Randy turned away. As soon as they did, my masochistic ear tuned in to Sarah, who was standing next to me, showing off the Scooby necklace to any alto chick who would listen. She was even wearing a red shirt with a cleavage-revealing neckline to accentuate the pendant. As she gushed on and on about how great Scooby was—

"He's taking me to the Z100 Jingle Ball! Front-row seats! How lucky am *I*?"

—I could feel the ticket I'd bought us for the Holiday Ball burning a hole through my wallet in my back pocket. Why I was still walking around with the thing, I had no idea. It was only a souvenir of shame, a monument to my dorkiness, proof positive of my ultimate loser status. I couldn't believe I wasted all that money on Sarah, who, it was becoming increasingly clear, couldn't have cared less about me.

"I'm going to the mall again today," Sarah explained, gazing down admiringly at the heart-shaped pendant. "Scooby has another gift for me. Isn't he just the best?"

The girls around Sarah oohed and aahed. How could I not have seen this before? Holly was right all along. All Sarah cared about were presents and cars and clothes and jewelry. That was why she was so focused on the gift aspect of Christmas and nothing else. That was why she was so psyched about my Jeep and why she'd stolen my sweater (which she'd yet to give back). That was why the first thing she'd asked me about after the fire was if I'd been able to save my *stuff*. I bet if I had handed her a credit card right then and there, she would have come right back to me. After making sure it had an inflated credit line, of course.

Sarah might have a few good qualities, but at heart

all she cared about was being the one with the most packages under the tree.

"Okay!" Mr. McDaniel said, clapping as he walked to the center of the room. "Let's get to work on 'The Twelve Days of Christmas'!" He turned and slid a piece of paper from the top of his piano, then scratched at his short red beard as he scanned the page. "Now, I've assigned all the different lines as solos to various students. We'll all sing the 'partridge in a pear tree' line together. Turk, I'd like you to take 'two turtledoves'; Danielle, 'three French hens'; Paul, 'four calling birds'; Sarah, I think you'll be perfect on 'five gold rings'. . . ."

Who better to sing about the only monetarily valuable item in the whole song? (There was a reason Jim Henson gave that line to Miss Piggy in *John Denver & the Muppets—A Christmas Together.*)

Well, let her have her little moment in the sun with her little song line. Suddenly I couldn't wait for that afternoon. Holly, the Hurley boys, and I were going to have some fun with the fabulous Scooby, and it would be all the more gratifying now that Sarah was going to be there to witness it.

That afternoon, as Matt and I walked toward the Hickory Farms kiosk, I told myself to just smile and try to be upbeat. But the second I saw my mother standing there in her reindeer costume, all I wanted to do was disappear. Could this be any more humiliating?

"Hey, Mrs. Nick!" Matt called out, walking up to her. "Can I get some of that Monterey Jack?"

Okay, so at least the outfit didn't faze *him.*

My mother's face lit up when she saw us. "Would

you like to try some, sir?" she asked me, holding out the tray as Matt munched on his second cube.

"This is good stuff, man. You should try it," he said, his cheek bulging.

"That's okay, Mom," I said. I'd just come from seeing my father, who was still in bad shape. Now I was confronted by the image of my mom as a furry reindeer in a green-and-red apron, and in five minutes I was going to be executing the next step in Project Scooby. My stomach was not well.

"So, how's your father?" she asked as a few elderly women took some cheese from the tray.

"He's . . . fine," I lied, my mind flashing on an image of my dad flat on his back on his bed, sipping a chocolate malt through a very long straw. He'd tried to act positive, but he could still barely move. It was tough to play along with the Dad's-just-fine game everyone else was so good at playing.

"The nurses only let us stay for five minutes, but he was joking the whole time. Same old Mr. Nick," Matt, who had been my taxi that afternoon, told her. "Your dad is so cool, man."

My mother smiled at this news, then looked at me with sympathy in her eyes. It looked kinda ridiculous over that big red nose she had on. "I know it's hard to see him like this, sweetie, but he's going to get better."

"Sure, Mom," I said, swallowing back a lump in my throat. I glanced at my watch conspicuously. "Well, better go. I'm gonna be late to meet Holly."

"I'm gonna go buy my mom's present," Matt said, stuffing another cube of cheese into his mouth. "Bye, Mrs. Nicholas. Later, bro."

He reached out and slapped my hand. "Thanks for the ride," I called after him as he melted into the crowd. I forced a smile at my mom. "I might be late tonight. I'm gonna study for the big history exam with the guys," I lied. I felt bad, but it wasn't like I had a choice. I couldn't tell my mom that I'd actually be on a crime spree with the Anti-Christmas Underground.

"Okay, sweetie," she said. "You have fun."

"Thanks," I replied. Then I turned and hoofed it toward the North Pole as fast as I could. Just looking at my mother made me feel guilty on so many levels, I couldn't even deal.

A few minutes later I was standing on the outskirts of the North Pole, behind the Santa Shack, watching Holly's slow trek through the mall as she tried to wrangle all six Hurley boys and keep from being mowed down by shoppers at the same time. Luckily the hyper, scary kids, at least one of whom always seemed to be beating up another, created a sort of buffer zone around her. No intelligent adult who valued his or her life would come within a five-foot radius.

"Hey!" Holly's face lit up, then fell when she saw me. "Where's the elf outfit? I brought a camera."

"No elf suit today. I'm gonna be Santa when Scooby's shift is over at five, remember? For now we're here strictly on a mission," I said as the smallest Hurley boy brought his foot down on the foot of another and got elbowed in the back of the head.

"This tool your boyfriend?" the eldest Hurley asked, offhandedly flicking one of his younger brothers on the ear. The response was a hard punch to the gut that the eldest didn't seem to notice. "What do you want with this guy when you can have a real man like me?" He lifted his chin slightly as he said this.

"Jason, you're nine," Holly said.

"So? I'm almost in the double digits," he replied, his steely blue eyes looking me up and down. I found myself irrationally wishing for a set of iron bars between us. He flicked another brother on the ear and the kid, never looking up from his Game Boy, kicked Jason on the shin, hard.

"Ow! You're gonna regret that!" Jason shouted, jumping the smaller kid. Suddenly all six boys piled on top of one another right there at our feet, a mass of flailing limbs and shouted curse words.

"Did you hear what he just said?" I asked Holly after one particularly harsh expletive flew our way.

"You should hear their mother," Holly replied. She reached in and grabbed one of the children by the back of his shirt, pulling him out of the pile as he continued to squirm and throw punches.

"Hey! Hey! Hey!" she shouted, then let out a loud peal of a whistle. "If you guys don't quit this right now, there's gonna be no Twinkies when we get home."

The pile froze and one by one the other five boys stood up and straightened their hodgepodge of sweatshirts and jackets. Holly was a miracle worker.

"Now, you guys wanna see Santa?" Holly asked in a cheerleadery tone I didn't know she possessed.

"Yeah!" they all cheered.

Of course, Jason couldn't help flicking the red-faced kid standing next to him and they immediately took off, tearing after each other across the center of the mall, trailing the rest of their brothers.

"Where are they going?" I asked. At this rate the Scooby plan was never going to get under way.

"They'll be back," Holly said with a shrug. Then a tiny woman with a bag twice her own size barreled right into Holly's shoulder and kept walking. Holly rolled her eyes and clenched her jaw. "Whaddaya say we sit?"

Holly walked past the mall's charity booth to find a place to rest and I felt all the hairs on my arms and neck stand on end. Every mall employee has to take one turn manning the charity booth and today it happened to be Marge Horvath's turn. As we strolled by, Marge glared right at me and lifted the right side of her upper lip in a kind of snarl. I glared right back.

"Ooh. What's *that* about?" Holly asked, noticing my face as we sat down on the outer rim of the pond at the center of the mall. "Isn't she that awful woman who sold us your Sarah necklace?"

I snorted. "Oh, that's her, all right. And she's not just awful, she's pure evil," I told Holly, shoving my hands into the pockets of my varsity jacket. "She hates my mother. She's the one who got her fired and I swear she was happy about it. I hate that woman."

"At least she's working the table for . . ." Holly squinted at the placard that was propped under the table. "Hope House. What's Hope House?"

"It's an orphanage. And she's only working there because she has to," I replied as we both watched Marge take a bill from an elderly man, grimacing when her fingers touched his.

At that moment the line of running Hurleys came tearing around the North Pole, and Jason ran right up to the big, rainbow-colored Hope House collection pot, shoved in his hand, and came out with a wad of bills.

"Jackpot!" he shouted gleefully.

That Awful Woman descended on him like a vulture on a ripe piece of meat. I didn't even see her move from her post and suddenly she was on Jason, clutching both his upper arms from behind and shaking him.

"You drop that money right where you found it, you little good-for-nothing terror!" she shouted, her face darkening and her eyes turning into nasty slits. In my mind's eye I suddenly saw a pair of horns sprout from her head and a roaring fire come to life behind her. Holly jumped up and ran over to Jason, forcibly removing the now subdued kid from Marge's grip.

"What's wrong with you? He's just a little boy," Holly said, smoothing down Jason's blond hair as he shakily dropped the money back into the pot.

"Well, I suggest you teach him to keep his hands to himself," Horvath snapped, her chin somehow seeming even pointier than usual. And that's pretty damn pointy.

Holly, her face pale, led Jason and the other boys over to me. "What do you say we go get in line?" she suggested.

"Yeah," I said, shooting Marge a look that she completely missed. She was too busy counting the money, transferring it from the pot to a tin where she could separate the bills. She was probably trying to make sure that Jason hadn't somehow managed to pocket a precious dollar. "Let's get the heck away from here."

*   *   *

By the time Holly had managed to get all six Hurleys in line for a visit with Santa, we were closing in on the end of Scooby's shift. I went into the Santa Shack to change into my Santa suit. Not wanting to miss the festivities, I kept glancing through the flimsy windowpanes of Plexiglas as I struggled into my suspenders and stuffed my padding under the waistband of my pants, marking the Hurleys' progress. The last thing I wanted was a repeat of yesterday's kerfuffle. (One of my mom's favorite words.)

As I pasted on my beard, I caught a glimpse of long blond hair down at the foot of the red carpet. My heart lurched, but I couldn't look away. There was Sarah, opening a brightly wrapped package. Her whole face lit up when she pulled out a deep purple cashmere sweater, letting the box and all the paper and ribbon fall all over the floor. She held the fabric up to her cheek, then bent down to whisper something to the little girl who was about to walk up to see Santa.

Where the hell did Scooby get the money to pay for all these presents? It wasn't like we made much bank playing Santa all day. And he couldn't be selling that many CDs, could he? Maybe his parents still gave him an allowance—like a hundred dollars a day. And it was tacky, the way he gave those presents to her in public so everyone could see how *generous* he was.

Sarah started to look up and I ducked away from the window, my pulse pounding. I didn't want her to catch me spying on her and think I was pining pathetically. I wasn't. Really.

"Hi, Santa," I heard the little girl say as she climbed onto Scooby's lap a few feet from the Santa Shack. "That pretty girl told me to tell you she loves the sweater."

"Well, thank you for the message, sweet thing," Scooby said. "How do you feel about rap music?"

I almost puked into my synthetic beard.

I peeked out the window again. The Hurleys were next and they were wrestling once more—all of them except the kid with the Game Boy, who was in a solid video game trance. Holly saw me and gave me a subtle thumbs-up. I smiled back hopefully. This had to work. It just had to. Scooby had to pay.

Soon the little girl was scurrying off and the smallest Hurley ran up the red carpet with inhuman speed.

"I'm first! I'm first!" he shouted.

This knocked Game Boy out of his trance. "Oh no you don't!" he shouted, chasing the youngest.

"Hey! I'm oldest! I get dibs!" Jason yelled.

In seconds Scooby had all six Hurley tanks hurtling toward him. From my vantage point, he might as well have been staring down the Giants' defense. I felt a chuckle building up in my throat. The taste of victory was so sweet.

"Whoa, whoa, whoa!" Scooby shouted, breaking character and standing up in an effort to defend himself.

"Aren't you supposed to say 'ho ho *ho*?'" Game Boy Hurley demanded, stopping in front of Scooby and holding his struggling brothers back.

"Uh . . . you kids are supposed to come up one at a time," Scooby said, tentatively returning to his throne.

"Yeah, well, we didn't," Jason informed him. "You got a problem with that, Fat Boy?"

I slapped a hand over my mouth to stop the laughter. The youngest Hurley curled and uncurled his fist menacingly. I couldn't have written this better myself.

"Okay, kids, why don't you all just take some free copies of my rap CD and go on your merry little ways?" Scooby suggested, leaning sideways to pull some CDs from the box he kept next to his chair. He handed one to Jason, who looked it over with interest.

"You rap?" Jason asked skeptically.

For a moment Scooby looked stricken. Revealing his true identity was totally verboten. Then, taking a hard look at his clearly curious audience, he cleared his throat. "Yeah, I do."

"Like what are some of your songs?" the second-to-littlest Hurley asked, rubbing snot from under his cold-reddened nose.

Scooby gave him a wink. "Wanna hear one?"

"Yeah!" they all cheered. And they sat down at Scooby's feet. Each one of them crossed his legs Indian style as if they were playing a giant game of Simon says. All I could do was look on in horrified awe.

> *My name is Santa and I'm da bomb!*
> *The ladies can't resist when I get my freak on!*
> *If ya never heard my rhymes, well, then too bad*
>   *for you,*
> *But I'm layin' down this track so you can hear me,*
>   *too!*
> *We got Santa over here,*
> *Santa over there,*
> *Santa on the mike,*
> *Santa everywhere!*

Okay, this was my worst nightmare come to life. And suddenly the Hurley boys started clapping,

keeping the beat for Scooby. People in line laughed
and bobbed their heads. Santa was putting on a show!
How novel! And he'd soothed the savage beasts that
had made their wait in line a living hell!

This was so, *so* wrong!

"No," I said under my breath, shaking my head.
"No! Nonononononononono! This isn't happening! This
isn't supposed to happen!"

And before I knew what I was doing, I had kicked
the wall of the Santa Shack in a blind fit of rage. And
it felt good. It felt damn good. Until I heard a
resounding crack. Then a pop. Then a really loud
creak. Then, right in front of my eyes, the wall of the
Santa Shack fell forward, then the left wall collapsed,
then the right, then the back wall, which, luckily, took
the roof with it. Otherwise I would have been a Paul
pancake. Scooby and the entire crowd fell silent as I
stood there in my Santa suit, my beard half attached
and my brown hair sticking up for all the world to see.

If I hadn't been so stunned, I probably would have
realized that right then was a good time to run.

"Santa! Who's that?" the youngest Hurley demanded,
pointing his pudgy little finger at me. He was clearly
traumatized by the sight of two Santas at once.

"Uh . . . I don't know," Scooby said in his Santa
voice. "He must be an imposter! Get him!"

The Hurleys scrambled to their feet and rushed
me, crushing the fallen Santa Shack walls beneath
their feet. *That* was when I actually started to run.

"You get back here, you fat fake!" one of the
Hurleys yelled.

I lumbered ahead as fast as I could, but with those

big boots and all that extra padding, I wasn't exactly able to reach my peak speed. I could feel them gaining on me, breathing down my neck. And suddenly one little body was thrown against me from behind and I sprawled on the dirty mall floor with just enough time to turn my head so that my nose didn't shatter.

"You're goin' down, imposter!" Jason shouted before throwing the first punch.

"Get off me!" I yelled.

I rolled over just in time to see my savior, Dale Dombrowski, head of mall security, hauling Hurleys off my body, his salt-and-pepper mustache twitching over a barely concealed smile. Dale was a good guy and I loved it when my mom retold his mall conspiracy theories to me and my dad over the dinner table. He was definitely going to love telling *this* story—the day he somehow managed, even with his aging muscles, to get four or five psychotic kids off of one scared would-be Santa. But try as he might, he couldn't get them all, and one of them was still pummeling my stomach quite vigorously. Luckily most of his punches were hitting my Santa padding.

"All right, kids, that's enough," Dale said, his tone calm, as if he held three squirming kids to his body every day of the week. "Leave Santa alone."

Holly's loud whistle split the air and the final combatants jumped off me, whirling to face her. She walked over and held out a hand, pulling me to my feet. My entire body ached and I was out of breath. The Hurleys' mom had better not be thinking about having more children. The world couldn't handle another.

"You okay?" Holly asked, her brow creased with concern. Funny. I thought she'd be laughing at me. Kind of like what Sarah and Scooby were doing at that very moment, standing over the crumbled pieces of the Santa Shack a few yards away.

"I'm fine," I told her.

"That's it," Holly spat at the boys. "No Twinkies for you!"

A general groan went up from her charges.

"All right, show's over," Dale said to curious passersby. "There's nothing to see here." He clucked his tongue and hoisted his waistband before reaching out and taking my arm. "Come on, kid, let's go get you patched up."

Dale led me over to the up escalator and the first-aid room on the second floor. I could feel my right eye swelling up a bit.

"That's right! Throw the lousy imposter in the clink!" Jason shouted after us, causing Sarah and Scooby to laugh even louder. All the kids waiting in line to see Scooby cheered. Plan B had officially tanked. I hung my head in shame as we ascended to the second floor. Where had I gone wrong?

And why, oh, *why* couldn't I get back at Scooby?

WHEN SANTA HITS THE GAS, MAN, JUST WATCH HER PEEL . . .

I WAS QUESTIONED BY MALL MANAGEMENT FOR HOURS. Apparently the Santa Shack had cost a pretty penny and they wanted to know what exactly had happened to bring the structure down. I, of course, lied through my teeth. If I'd told them the truth, I would have had to pay for it, and we are already well versed in my negative cash flow situation. Mr. Papadopoulos, his head shining under the fluorescent lights, seemed skeptical that I had leaned against the wall while putting on my Santa boots and it had collapsed, but he finally let me go.

As I passed by the glass wall of his office, I caught a glimpse of my murky reflection. Mr. Papa-D had respectfully asked me not to return to work until my face had fully healed. (Apparently a Santa who looked like he'd lived through a gang war was unacceptable.) I had a nice shiner forming around my right eye and there was a bit of dried blood under the Band-Aid over my left. When I touched my face, I winced in pain and then felt a rush of angry adrenaline. This was all Scooby's fault. I couldn't believe he'd managed to turn the Hurleys on me. Why was he so untouchable?

I walked over to the railing around the food court and leaned my forearms against it, looking down at the scene below. The North Pole had been closed for the night so that the Santa Shack could be rebuilt. Shoppers were pausing to stare at the destruction as they walked by, and there stood Scooby, right next to the fallen walls, wearing a red-and-black flannel shirt and black jeans, talking to some young guy in a suit. They were laughing and pointing and yukking it up. Even from here I could see that Adam's apple bounce. For Scooby, it was all just a funny story that was probably growing in hilarity with every retelling. Meanwhile I could feel my bruises swelling every moment.

There was a slight bulge in the back pocket of my jeans of which I suddenly became very aware. Something I'd taken from my practical joke box that morning as an afterthought. I'd only brought it along in case of an emergency. I'd never used it before in my life and I never really thought I would. I never thought I'd find someone I hated enough to test it on.

But now I had.

I headed to McDonald's, purchased a Super Size fries, and pulled the little packet out of my jeans pocket. On the surface of the white package was a picture of a rotund cartoon kid with green bubbles floating away from his backside. Over his head were the words *Ultimate Gaspiration* in big purple letters. At that moment, those two words were my salvation. I emptied the entire packet of powder over the fries, shook them up for good measure, and hopped on the escalator. I never took my eyes off Scooby as I descended.

As I approached, Scooby and his cohort turned to look at me.

"Is this the guy?" the suited man asked, a gleeful smile on his face as he looked me over.

"This is the guy," Scooby said, laughing.

I barely registered the fact that they had been talking about me. All I could see was green bubbles. I held the fries out to Scooby.

"Gotcha something to eat," I said. "Just to show there's no hard feelings."

"I hate McDonald's fries," Scooby said, frowning and crossing his arms over his chest.

"What?" the suited man and I asked in baffled unison.

What was this guy, some kind of alien?

"I'll take 'em," the suited man said.

He had the fries out of my hand and had shoved a wad of them into his mouth before I even got over the shock that somebody didn't like McDonald's fries. As far as I was concerned, they were the fifth major food group.

"Ugh! *So* good," the suited man said. That was when I snapped out of it and realized what he was doing.

"Hey! Don't eat—"

"Yo! Christopher!"

Two large men walked up and set down a ton of camera equipment next to the suited man's feet. They were soon joined by a frenzied woman who was wearing headphones too big for her small head. Her frizzy black hair stuck up all around her head like a lion's mane and she was wearing lipstick the color of grape bubble gum.

"Hey, guys! We all set?" Christopher asked, his mouth full.

"Yeah, we got permission to film," the woman answered, holding one hand over one side of her headphones. "But we got to get the shot set up fast. We're going live in a few minutes."

"Is this the guy?" the bigger man said, scratching at his itchy beard as he lifted his chin at me.

"This is the guy," Christopher replied, shoveling fries into his mouth.

"What *guy*?" I asked, irritated by the refrain.

"The guy who destroyed the Santa Shack," the woman said as if I were completely exasperating. "Didn't Christopher tell you? He's going to interview you on the air. We're from News Twelve. We want you on the live six o'clock broadcast."

Wait a second, they wanted to interview *me*? *Live?* With a black eye? While the reporter was ingesting a carton full of power laxative? I glanced over at Scooby, who was watching me intently. I swear for a second there I felt like he could read my mind. God, I hated him.

But I couldn't focus on that now. I had to get out of this. I had to—

"Okay, black-eye kid, you stand on Christopher's left," the little woman said, grabbing me by both arms and shoving me up next to Christopher. "Lumberjack kid, you stand to Christopher's right," she said, manhandling Scooby as well.

I felt like my heart was going to pound right through my chest. The large men trained the camera on us and I wiped my palms on my jeans, staring at the dwindling number of fries in Christopher's carton. He was starting to slow down, but he was still eating. This poor guy. He had no idea what was about to happen.

"Nervous?" he asked, letting out a little belch.

"Uh . . . kind of," I said. Scooby, of course, laughed.

"Have a fry, you'll feel better," Christopher told me. When he held out the carton to me, my stomach lurched. Green gas bubbles danced in my head.

"Uh . . . I don't think so," I replied, stuffing my hands under my arms. My black eye started to throb and I felt prickly sweat forming along my hairline.

"Come on, have one," Christopher said.

"No . . . no, really." I took a step back.

"What's the problem, loser?" Scooby asked, looking over Christopher's head at me. There was a suspicious glint in his eyes. "Why don't you want to eat them?"

All of a sudden a wave of realization came over me. Scooby knew something was up. And if I didn't eat at least one fry, his suspicions would be confirmed. And when Christopher went running for the bathroom, Scooby would *know* I'd done something to the fries and then the frantic producer lady would call the police and I'd be arrested for giving the News 12 reporter food poisoning, I'd be pegged as a delinquent, and they'd know I took down the Santa Shack not entirely by mistake. I was going to jail. And then I'd never get back at Scooby.

"Fine," I said. "Thanks."

I took one fry—a small one—said a little prayer, and popped it into my mouth.

"Huh," Christopher said. "I don't feel so good."

He placed the fry carton on the ground at his feet and came up holding his hand over his stomach. I swallowed with difficulty. *Just don't let him get sick on the air. Just don't let him get sick on the air—*

"And we're going live in five, four, three, two . . ."

The woman pointed at us, the red light went on over the camera, and Christopher let out the loudest, longest fart imaginable. And I used to bunk under Fat Willy after he ate four sloppy joes at dinner back in camp. There was a moment of silence, then the smell came, and then Scooby collapsed in convulsive laughter.

"Uh . . . this is News Twelve field reporter Christopher Wallace, coming to you live from Paramus Park mall in Paramus, New Jersey, where tonight, shoppers witnessed a Christmas tragedy of sorts—"

Pppppptthhhhhhhhllllllllttttt!

Scooby was crouched to the floor, one hand braced on the linoleum, the other arm over his stomach as he laughed. His Adam's apple bulged dangerously. Christopher was sweating buckets and seemed to be scanning the area for a method of escape. The producer woman held her nose. She was turning red, but she waved her free hand frantically at Christopher, trying to get him to talk. Amazingly, Christopher continued.

"Dozens of children were in line to see Santa Claus when they heard a terrifying noise—"

Pppppttthhhllllllaaaaatt! Phlat . . . pppt . . . pppt . . . ppppt!

My stomach shifted dangerously. Between the smell that was now thick in the air, my nerves, and my own french fry starting to work its magic, I felt like I was about to throw up.

"Uh . . . *Paul!*" Christopher practically shouted my name in desperation as he turned to me. He bent slightly at the waist, clearly trying to . . . well . . . hold things together. "Why don't you tell us what happened here tonight?"

Phhhlllloooot!

That time it was me.

Scooby pulled himself into a fetal position on the floor, laughing uncontrollably. The guys behind the camera were almost choking. The producer threw up her hands and turned away.

"Okay, this is Christopher Wallace, signing off," Christopher said. He waved his hand at the cameramen, his eyes bulging. Somehow he waited until the red light went off. Then he ran. My stomach, now a mass of shifting bubbles, told me to follow and so I did, running as fast as I could, leaving a noxious trail of green bubbles behind me.

"Go! Go! Go!" Dirk whisper-shouted later that night from his lookout spot behind the train station in the center of Montvale. Rudy and I emerged from the bushes across Grand Avenue, the awkward, seven-foot-tall plastic Santa balanced between us. We hightailed it across the street and chucked the Santa into the back of Ralph's Toyota pickup, where it landed with a crack on top of seven other Santas.

My stomach instantly cramped up and I doubled over just as Rudy tried to high-five me. He caught air and nearly threw himself off his feet. Dirk rushed out from behind the train station and jumped into the passenger seat of the truck.

"Paul, what are you doing? Get in the car!" Holly demanded, leaning out the window of her Bug. A car raced by, but luckily they didn't seem interested in the fact that there were two vehicles in the train station's handicapped lot at one o'clock in the morning.

The truck peeled out and Rudy and I lurched toward the VW, gravel shifting under our feet. Rudy stuffed himself into the backseat next to Flora, and I slumped into the front and slammed the door.

"Are you okay?" Holly asked, pedal to the metal to catch up with Ralph.

"Fine," I replied. I didn't feel the need to tell her that I'd taken twenty Pepto-Bismol pills since six o'clock and was now fairly certain that I was never going to have another bowel movement for the rest of my life. I couldn't believe the effects of one fry! And poor Christopher Wallace had been hospitalized for dehydration. I was officially a menace to society.

"Whooooo!" Rudy shouted in the backseat, raising his fists. "How great was that? We are the anti-Christmas *kings*!"

He raised his hand for another high five and looked at us hopefully. Holly was driving and I was moping, so Flora finally leaned forward a bit, slapped his hand, and then sat back to look out the window again.

"What's *wrong* with you people?" Rudy demanded. "We kick butt! Don't you love how it feels to kick butt?"

"Yeah!" Holly said with a laugh, now that we were speeding along Kinderkamack Road with no police lights flashing in the rearview. "Santa is *history*!"

Rudy whooped in joy and I looked at Holly out of the corner of my eye. She smiled over at me, but when she saw my face, her forehead creased. She stopped at a red light and put the car into neutral.

"What is up with you, Nicholas?" she asked, tucking her hair behind her ear. "You've been out of it all night."

"I just don't get it," I replied, flicking the heat vent

open and closed. "It's like Scooby has some kind of personal force field."

Holly let out a sigh and shoved the gearshift into first as the light turned green. "Will you get over it already?" she asked, focused on the road. "Scooby is just one guy. We just pulled off a major act of anti-Christmas mayhem here! Seven town Santas! I mean, come on, Paul!"

"Yeah!" Rudy shouted, grabbing the back of my seat and leaning forward so that his smiley face was right next to mine. "We rule!"

I couldn't help smiling back at him. Rudy is one of those infectious-energy guys. "You're right," I said, sitting up. I watched the Santa bodies bouncing up and down in the bed of Ralph's truck up ahead. "Christmas is going down, baby! Yeah!"

"Whooo-hoo!" Rudy shouted. He looked at Flora. "Come on, say it one time with me—"

"Whooo-hoo!" they both shouted again.

Holly laughed and turned on the radio, loud, and we sped back through the deserted streets of Washington Township, rapping along to P. Diddy at the top of our lungs. By the time we piled out of the car in Dirk's driveway, my mind-set had readjusted. I was elated. Euphoric, really. Here I was with my best friend in the world, along with all these new friends, and we had just pulled off a serious rebel act without getting caught. I wasn't sure if I'd ever done anything rebellious before in my life. It was kind of . . . freeing.

Ralph and Dirk started to unload the Santas, leaning them against the side of the truck like a North Pole police lineup. As Ralph sat the last Santa down on the ground—a hollow plastic one with a chipping face and a faded red suit that had clearly been used for one too many seasons, I felt a surge of hatred course through me. As I stared at the Santa, its bulbous face suddenly morphed into Scooby's laughing one.

Laughing. Always laughing.

I looked at Dirk. He twitched and smirked, like he knew what I was thinking.

I pulled back my fist and sank it right into Scooby's nose. His entire face collapsed around my hand and everyone cheered. It felt very, very good.

And suddenly I was completely exhausted.

"I think it's time to go home," Holly said, putting her arm around my shoulders.

"Are you kidding? We're on a roll here!" Dirk said, his head twitching violently to the side so that his ear almost touched his shoulder.

"Yeah! A roll!" Rudy exploded, bouncing up and down like a boxer.

"What else you got for us, Dirk?" Ralph asked. He leaned his head back slightly so that his neck seemed to disappear.

Dirk's eyes slid left and right, taking in the little circle of followers that was gathered around him, the steam from our breath mingling in the air. Suddenly all the hair on the back of my neck stood on end. There was a new, disturbing vibe rushing between all of us.

One twitch, then Dirk spoke. "I happen to know where they're keeping all the floats for the Wooddale Christmas parade," he said.

Flora's eyes lit up and Rudy let out an "Awww, yeah!"

I glanced at Holly and her eyes mirrored mine. The Wooddale Christmas parade? It was a tradition. It was an institution. It was a joyous event my parents and I had attended together every year since birth. People came from all over the area to watch the parade down Wooddale Avenue. Kids from local dance schools would dress up as elves and sugarplum fairies and dance down the street. A brass band played Christmas carols. Santa had a new and more elaborate float every year and Mrs. Claus would throw candy into the crowd from the seat next to his. There was a Hanukkah float and a Kwanza float and a float with the baby New Year. They even had real reindeer. I'd never missed a Wooddale parade in my life.

And Holly used to come with us. Until a couple of years ago, of course. It had always been one of the most happy, Christmassy nights of the year. We'd watch the parade, go out for hot chocolate afterward, drive around looking at light displays. . . .

"You in, Paulie?" Dirk asked. The way he said my name always made me feel like I was an extra on *The Sopranos*.

Ralph, Rudy, and Flora all looked at me with anticipation. My heart turned in my chest. Stealing decrepit Santas was one thing, but could I really take down the Wooddale parade?

"You don't have to do this," Holly told me quietly.

But when I looked into Dirk's eyes, I knew I did. These people were my friends. My brethren. *Mi amigos.* They were helping me deal with Scooby. They'd taken me in when I felt like my whole world was falling apart. I couldn't let them down now. I had to show anti-Christmas solidarity. Besides, it wasn't like my family was going to make it to the parade this year—not with my father in Christmas-mishap traction. I glanced at the deflated face of my Scooby stand-in Santa and nodded.

"I'm in," I said.

My heart in my throat, I climbed into the cab of Ralph's truck with Dirk. He clapped his hand on my shoulder like a proud Godfather and we headed off to Wooddale.

DON WE NOW
OUR GAY APPAREL

As I WALKED THROUGH THE ICU ON FRIDAY MORNING, I got more than a few disturbed looks from the nurses on duty. Not that I could blame them. My cut had closed up, but my shiner was rather shiny, I was sporting a bit of stubble, and my eyes were bloodshot. Add that to the fact that I was still wearing my rumpled, dirt-stained jeans from the night before and that I hadn't even been home since our anti-Christmas adventures, and I probably looked like a crack addict who'd wandered in off the street.

But there was still an hour to kill before school and I wasn't sure I was going to get to see my dad later. Besides, I'd just spent hours sabotaging the Wooddale Christmas parade—only my father's favorite out-of-house tradition. The guilt was killing me. Maybe chilling with my father for a while would make it ease up a little.

I walked over to the doorway to my father's room and stood there for a moment, my mouth completely dry. Dad was staring toward the window on the far side of the room, the blinds drawn across it. He hadn't seen me yet and that gave me a chance to find my voice and figure out what to say. My state of total exhaustion made standing there looking at my weakened, prone father even more difficult. I still couldn't believe this was happening, but the eyes didn't lie. My dad was lying there wearing a thin cotton gown, he was hooked up to at least three machines, and his skin was as waxy as a surfboard.

When I felt tears prickling my eyes, I cleared my throat. "Hey, Dad."

He turned his head, winced, then turned it more slowly. At least he could move a little more now. That was an improvement over the last time I'd been here. His entire face lit up when he saw me. Well, as much as it could, considering how difficult it still was for him to move his face muscles. His eyes twinkled for a second, then darkened.

"Son! What happened to you?" he asked.

My hand flew to my black eye. "Oh, these kids at the mall didn't like my Santa impression," I told him, stepping tentatively into the room. Not exactly a lie. "Don't worry. It's not as bad as it looks." Actually, it was worse than it looked, but who was I to complain? The man was being forced to use a bedpan, for Christmas' sake! (I really have to break myself of that phrase now that I'm anti-Christmas.)

"I'm glad you're here," my father said, reaching for the remote attached to the bed. He hit a button and the mechanism whined to life, pushing my father into a seated position. His face turned red and I could tell the movement was painful for him, but he was trying not to let it show.

All this because of a stupid Christmas lights mishap.

"Your mother tells me you slept at a friend's last night?" he asked.

"Yeah," I replied. That was the story I'd told my mom when I'd called her from the cab of Ralph's truck to tell her I wouldn't be coming home. Of course I *had* been with friends all night, but sleep hadn't been part of the festivities.

"I understand why you might not want to be home," my father said. "I know the house is a mess—your mother told me about your room. . . ."

I looked down at my muddy Pumas. I sensed a guilt trip coming on.

"But Paul, your mother really needs you, especially without me there," my father said, causing my chest to ache. "And I'd really like it if you'd at least put up a few strands of new lights . . . maybe around the doors and windows," he continued. "Just so the kids who come by won't be too upset. And I also think it would cheer your mother up a bit—start getting things back to normal."

I glanced at my father to see if he was being ironic, but no. His face was quite serious—even hopeful. Who was he kidding? Things were never going to be back to normal.

"I know I can count on you, Paul. I'm so glad that you're full of the Christmas spirit. I think it's really going to help you get through this," my father said, expending some serious energy to move his hand toward me.

I sat down in the chair next to his bed and put my

hand on top of his. My heart felt like it was ripping
open. My poor, delusional father. My Christmas *spirit*
was going to help me through this? What were they
doing in this place, spoon-feeding him hallucinogens?
Christmas was the cause of all our misery! If anything,
my father should see that more clearly than anyone
else. He was the one lying here practically paralyzed
with needles sticking out of his arms! All because the
Christmas spirit had turned *against* us.

"So, you'll help your mother decorate the house?"
my father asked, his voice growing harsh. I could tell
this conversation was taking a lot out of him.

"Yeah, Dad," I told him, even though I could
think of nothing I'd less like to do. "I will."

"Everybody's staring at my eye," I said to Holly as
I followed her toward our usual lunch table on Friday
afternoon.

Turk and Randy were standing a few tables away
and they bent their heads together, talking as they looked
me over. Turk said something to Dinuka Samarasinghe
and he turned in his seat to check me out. I might as
well have had the words *Kindergartners' Punching Bag*
tattooed across my forehead.

"That's because I told them you got it fighting off
a gang that tried to hold up Krauser's last night,"
Holly said, swinging her hair behind her shoulders as
she sat down next to Marcus.

My mouth dropped open in awe. "You are my
hero," I told her.

"I'm aware," she said gleefully, stealing a fry from
my tray.

"Wait, so it's not true?" Matt said, joining her in her fry poaching. "I've been telling everybody!"

"Please, like Paul could beat up a gang by himself," Marcus said with a scoff as he brought his burger to his mouth. "It was probably a couple of fifth graders lifting gum."

"Whatever, dude. You weren't there," I said, the heat rising in my face. He was just a little too close to being on the nose with his assessment.

I sat down and pulled my wallet out of my back pocket. I'd dropped my change on the tray as always and when I went to put it back in my billfold, I could barely jam the few dollars in there.

"You really need to clean that thing out," Holly said, grabbing a few more of my fries.

"I'm aware," I shot back. I pulled the rather large, white Holiday Ball ticket out of the billfold and tossed it unceremoniously onto the table. Then I shoved the money in and sat down. Holly was looking at the elaborately lettered ticket and trying to look like she wasn't.

"Okay, let me have it," I told her, reaching for a french fry. The moment I picked one up, my stomach rumbled dangerously and I put it down again. What had I been thinking, ordering fries?

"Let you have what?" Holly asked.

"I know you want to slam me for wasting my money on that thing," I told her, lifting my chin and crossing my arms over my chest. "Give me your best shot."

Holly shrugged and took a bite of her burger. "Actually, I was just kind of surprised you still had it."

"Yeah, you're not still going, are you?" Matt asked. "We're playing poker at Marc's tonight."

"We are?" I asked.

"Yeah," Marcus said. "You're bringing the jerky. Didn't you get my e-mail?"

"Dude, my computer currently has the consistency of Cheez Whiz," I said.

"Sorry," Marcus said, raising his hands. "Are you in or what?"

"Yeah," I said. "I guess."

I picked up my grape soda, and my eyes naturally traveled across the cafeteria to the table where Sarah had been sitting all week, ever since our breakup. Morosely I wondered which mystery cafeteria dish she was trying out today. Or maybe she'd given in to the habits of the girls at her table and was only eating salad and drinking water. Not-so-lovingly nicknamed the Hair Spray Table, it was home to some of the wealthiest, snobbiest, bitchiest females of our time. Sarah was sandwiched between Britney White and Britney Stein, wearing her new Scooby cashmere. Lainie Lefkowitz pointed to something in the pages of a glossy magazine and they all squealed, laughed, and high-fived. Everyone except Sarah. She merely smiled and sipped her milk. Milk. Good. Her inability to fully immerse herself in their behavioral patterns made my heart pang—at least she was still her own person.

Of course, after everything that had happened, I wasn't sure I knew who that person was. I tore my eyes away. What was the point?

The two things you do *know are that she's materialistic and she's a Scooby lover. Just remember that,* I told myself.

"Look, Paul . . . if you still want to go . . . ," Holly

was saying as I took a gulp of my soda, "I'll go with you."

I snorted in surprise and grape soda came right out my nose. Matt and Marcus cracked up laughing and Matt slapped me on the back.

"Ugh! Get a trough!" Holly said, pushing herself away from the table. I scrambled for a napkin and held it under my nose. The pain was excruciating. You really don't want to send sugar and bubbles up your nasal passages. It's not a fun sensation.

"Are you kidding me?" I said through the flimsy napkin, which was now stained purple.

"Yeah, Stevenson," Marcus said. "You're not exactly a school dance kinda girl."

"Really, Marc? Then what kind of girl *am* I?" Holly asked, leveling him with a glare.

"You know, the tackle football kind of girl," Marcus replied, unfazed.

Holly blinked. She had been known to play tackle football with us on occasion. "Okay, true," she said. She gazed down at the Holiday Ball ticket. "But it could be kind of cool."

Kind of cool? This had to be a joke. The thought of Holly at a Holiday Ball was wrong on so many levels. The anti-Christmas level, the joiner level, the girly level . . .

"Do you even own a dress?" I blurted out, dropping my hand away from my face.

Matt and Marcus laughed again. Holly picked up a fry and tossed it at my forehead, where it bounced off and landed in her Jell-O.

"Come on!" she said, her green eyes dancing. "It could be fun to get dressed up and act like a normal human being for once. Besides, you already paid for it. And you practically organized the whole thing! Don't you want to see how it turns out?"

She had a point there. I *had* worked my butt off on the plans for this shindig, painstakingly ensuring that anything that had gone wrong at the last three balls would not be repeated. We'd splurged on a caterer to avoid being fed reheated lunch food, we'd ordered an extra helium tank so that everyone could suck the gas to their heart's content during setup and we still wouldn't run out like we had last year, and I'd hand-picked all the chaperones. (Turk Martin's uncle had volunteered two years in a row and had hit on the head cheerleaders both times. Not pretty.)

I looked down at the ticket and realized all at once that there was no reason why we shouldn't go.

"Sorry, guys," I said, glancing at Matt. "You're gonna have to get your own jerky."

"Yeah?" Holly said, raising her eyebrows.

I started to smile and looked up at her, the inside of my nose and throat still stinging. "Yeah," I said. "Let's do it."

Holly grinned and I felt something I hadn't felt in days. I actually felt kind of happy.

"Oh, Paul, you look so handsome!" my mother told me, giving my tie a little tweak as we stood in the front hallway.

Her face was practically gleaming with pride and I didn't have the heart to point out the big purple-and-yellow stain around my eye. The swelling had gone down, but the colors had shifted and I now looked like some kind of deranged Batman villain. Huh. That could actually be kind of cool. I could be the freak that Christmas had wronged, taking out my pain on all of society. But what would I be called . . . ? The Christmas Revenger? The Jingler? The Snowblower?

"I'm so glad to see you getting back into the spirit of things," my mother told me. "I was worried about you for a few days there."

I forced a smile and bit my tongue. It wasn't like I was going to stand there and tell her that this was a fluke. That I wasn't actually in any spirit of any kind. That Holly and I would probably last half an hour before all of the Christmas carols and mighty-good-cheer irritated us to the point of insanity and we had to make our escape.

"Did you hear about the Santa robberies last night?" my mother asked suddenly, her hand fluttering to her throat. "It's so horrible. Seven towns lost their town Santas. Can you imagine the type of person who would do such a thing?"

You're lookin' at him, my brain said, and I felt my cheeks flush with the secret.

"I gotta go, Mom," I told her, turning away before she could read my face. "Thanks for letting me borrow the car."

"Anytime, sweetie!" my mother called after me as I jogged down the path toward the driveway. Her chipper, happy, trusting voice made my shoulders curl forward. What would my mother think if she found out that her precious Christmas-loving son was exactly the type of evil Santa-stealing person she couldn't even imagine? The guilt settled in hard on my shoulders as I waved to her, still standing in the open doorway, before pulling out. What was I doing? Was all this anti-Christmas stuff worth losing the respect of my parents?

Don't think that way, the little voice in my head told me as I drove toward Holly's house. *Christmas has forsaken you. You can't feel guilty about forsaking it right back.*

By the time I pulled up at the foot of Holly's curving driveway, I was a mess of frayed nerves. A battle was being waged in my head between the old Paul and the new, and my eye was starting to throb. Maybe this Holiday Ball thing had been a huge mistake. Did I really want to immerse myself in an elaborate Christmas party after I'd spent last night waging war against the holiday?

I was so thoroughly confused that I leaned on the horn extra hard and extra long, trying to get out some of my aggression. I was deciding how to bail on this whole thing when the front door of Holly's house opened, and every last one of my warring thoughts went out the window.

Holly was standing there in a floor-length black velvet gown with a high neck and no sleeves. She had some sort of cape or wrap thingie draped over her shoulders. Her hair was pulled back with a few curls dangling around her face. Even from this distance I could tell she was wearing some kind of glittery makeup that made her whole face sparkle. And lipstick. The girl was wearing lipstick.

I actually reached my hands up to rub my eyes but mercifully remembered my injuries at the last second. It didn't matter, anyway. Holly was approaching the car now and there was no denying it. She looked gorgeous. She looked . . . sexy. My best friend was capable of sexiness.

Holly opened the car door and lowered herself into the seat, tucking her high heels under the hem of her dress. The whole car filled with an unfamiliar flowery scent. She slammed the door, reached over, and touched my chin. It took a second for me to realize that she was pushing my mouth closed.

"You gonna drive?" she asked, grinning.

"You look . . ."

"I'm aware," she said, blushing slightly.

She turned and faced forward and I put the car in drive. This was going to be a very interesting night.

"I gotta hand it to you, Paul, this is the coolest dance I've ever been to," Holly said, fiddling with the stem of her plastic champagne flute.

"Hol, it's the only dance you've ever been to," I pointed out.

"Point taken," Holly said.

She sipped her sparkling cider and looked out across the dance floor. For the millionth time that night I found myself staring at her in disbelief. Was this really my tomboy best friend? She looked even more beautiful in the dim light cast by the twinkling white Christmas tree strands that were draped all over the gym. And it wasn't just me. At least ten people had gone mute when they saw her.

"How did you get all the trees?" Holly asked.

"My dad cut a deal with the manager at Treasure Island," I replied, trying without much luck to stifle a proud grin.

However anti-Christmas I was feeling, I had to take at least one moment to revel in my success. People had been coming up to me all night telling me how amazing the gym looked. The walls under the basketball nets were lined with fake evergreens and we'd bought a couple of dozen cans of aerosol fir tree scent so that the room smelled authentic. Silver, white, and clear balloons packed the ceiling, with curly silver ribbons dangling down from each one. The refreshment tables were draped with garlands and paper Hanukkah and Christmas decorations. But my favorite touch was the tableau set up around the DJ's table in the corner. The art club had been commissioned to make life-size cardboard replicas of the entire *Peanuts* gang, singing around the pathetic little tree that Charlie Brown brings home.

I always thought that particular TV special really brought home the meaning of Christmas. It was a holiday that made everything beautiful.

I looked at Holly and she smiled. Yeah. *Everything* was made beautiful.

But not anymore, the little voice in my head pointed out.

I looked down at the silver-and-white tablecloth. Out of nowhere I felt very heavy and very sad. Like my best friend had just dumped me and left me forever. But that was ridiculous. It was just a holiday. I was practically an adult here. It was going to have to stop being magical sometime, right?

"Hey," Holly said suddenly. "Wanna dance?"

My heart skipped a beat in surprise. A slow song had just started up and groups of people were moving toward the walls while all the school's established couples went to the dance floor.

"You want to . . . dance?" I asked. *With me?* my

brain added silently. This was a contingency I hadn't planned for. We were only supposed to stick this thing out for half an hour, and I never thought Holly would want to actually dance. This was a girl who would rather watch *The NFL Today* than *TRL*.

"Come on," she said, standing. "It's my first dance. We might as well . . . you know, *dance* at it."

"Okay," I said, fumbling to wipe off my appetizer-greased fingers as I stood.

I followed Holly over to the middle of the dance floor, hundreds of pairs of eyes marking our progress. I knew what everyone was thinking. We'd been teased since the third grade about being a couple. They all probably figured we'd finally given in to the inevitable. People were so stupid. Right. Me and Holly. Together. Ha!

Holly stopped and turned to me and I paused for a moment, my heart in my throat. Suddenly I couldn't remember what to do with my hands. This was Holly. Was I really supposed to . . . *hold* her?

She slipped her arms around my neck and there was nothing I could do but lace my hands together around her waist. I was as stiff as a corpse and there were about two feet between us. I methodically moved back and forth to the music, starting to sweat. What was wrong with me? It wasn't like *I'd* never been to a dance before.

"Are you okay?" Holly asked me. As she spoke, she inched a bit closer to me. My heart lurched, but then I realized it was actually better—more comfortable. I could bend my arms. I started to feel a little less awkward.

"I'm fine," I said.

"Paul, I—"

"What?" I asked.

"Nothing," she said, looking away.

"Oh no!" I said. "Remember the Pact! That time you *did* start a sentence!"

"Forget it, okay?" she said, struggling to hold back a smile.

"No way! You would *kill* me if I went back on the Pact," I said, laughing.

"Paul," she said, turning her face toward mine again.

Something in her voice cut my laughter short. For the first time since we hit the dance floor, I looked into her eyes. An intense tingling feeling dropped from my heart all the way down through my toes.

Holly was giving me the Look.

The look someone gives you when they want you to kiss them. Eyelids kinda heavy. Green eyes somehow more intensely green. An unspeakable heat rushed over my skin and now my whole body was sweating under my suit.

Oh. My. God. She was going to do it. She was going to *kiss* me! How was this possible? And why, why, *why* was I suddenly thinking about my breath? It wasn't like I was actually going to let this happen, was I?

Holly leaned in a little closer to me and my eyes started to close. I *was* going to let this happen, apparently.

In fact, from the beating of my heart I was starting to realize it might not be a half-bad idea.

Before I knew it, I was leaning closer to her, closing the gap between us. Our lips were about to touch. I was about to kiss Holly Stevenson. And then—

"AAAAAAAHHHHHHHHH! Gross! Oh my God! GROSS!"

Holly and I jumped apart and everyone else on the dance floor stopped as well. It was Sarah's voice, and in the midst of the confusion I realized that I actually hadn't thought about her all night. There was another shriek, followed by another, and then a bunch of people over by the Secret Santa table backed up as if they were trying to get away from something. They were all looking at the floor, and I saw a couple of girls turn their faces away and hide them in their boyfriends' jacket lapels.

"What's going on?" Holly asked.

"Scooby! This isn't funny!" Sarah's strained voice carried across the gym.

The crowd around the table parted enough for us to see Sarah, in a white strapless minidress, standing over a few crushed boxes on the gym floor. Scooby was next to her, wearing what I assume he thought was a pimped-out purple tux, holding his stomach and laughing.

I looked at Holly and we both shrugged.

"Sarah, what is it? What's wrong?" asked Mr. McDaniel, one of our chaperones.

"Look!" Sarah wailed, pointing at the boxes on the floor. For the first time I noticed a smear of brown on one of her white shoes. "Someone replaced all the Secret Santa gifts with . . . *dog poo*!"

And with that, Sarah burst into uncontrollable sobs and flung herself into Mr. McDaniel's arms. He patted her back and inched her away from the mess as Scooby grasped a chair for support. A resounding "ewww!" went out across the gym and everyone made their way toward the far wall. Coach Bullock, the football coach, started wrangling some of his team to dispose of the unopened gifts and start cleaning up the mess.

"I don't believe it," Holly said suddenly, a laugh in her voice.

"What?" I asked. I think I was still in shock.

"Look over by the equipment room," Holly said, covering her mouth.

I glanced over without moving my head and saw Dirk peeking out the equipment room door. We locked eyes and Dirk suddenly twitched.

"Ew! Ewww! *EEEEEEWWW!*" Lainie Lefkowitz shrieked as the janitor mopped up the poo, momentarily widening the smear.

I laughed and shook my head at Dirk in wonder. He and the other members of the Anti-Christmas Underground emerged from the equipment room in formal gear, blending in perfectly with the students and their dates. Then they quickly and unobtrusively slipped out the side door.

"Classic," Holly said.

They're Singing "Deck the Halls," but It's Not Like Christmas at All . . .

When I woke up on Saturday morning, I had no idea where I was. There was a lot of loud banging and gruff voices shouting and then something mechanical and totally inappropriate for morning operation whirred to life right outside my window. I wrenched my eyes open. All I could see was a mishmash of pastel. My forehead was pressed up against something hard, which was weird because my bed isn't next to a wall. I blinked a few times, pulled back, and realized that I was on the pullout couch in the den and that I had slept right up against one of the arms of said couch. I reached up to feel my forehead and found the bumpy, crisscrossed imprint of the plaid couch fabric on my skin.

Someone walked by the window, startling me, and when I turned my head, a sharp pain slashed through my eyeball. I slapped my hand over my eye and saw, with the other one, a couple of big men in quilted coats, leaning a ladder against the house. The workmen. Right. But it was Saturday. Didn't construction guys ever get a break?

I tried to lie down, but another stabbing eye pain killed that fantasy. *Ow!*—then it sliced through my head. And my neck. Ugh! What kind of freaky position had I slept in?

I sat up, rubbing my neck, and my eyes fell on the desk chair in the corner of the room. My suit jacket was flung over the back of it and my red tie had slipped to the floor during the night, where it sat in a little coiled pile.

Right. The Holiday Ball was last night. And afterward Holly and I had gone out to the diner with the rest of the Underground and gorged ourselves on cheese fries. And the night before that was spent running around destroying Christmas with no sleep to speak of. No wonder I'd slept all night in a weird position. My body was probably too tired to move. When I'd gotten home, I'd been so drained I'd practically collapsed. I hadn't even walked Holly to her door when I dropped her off, a breach of etiquette that would send my mother's mind reeling if she ever found out.

Holly.

"Oh *no!*" I said, my voice scratchy and dry. I brought my hands up to cover my face and tried to squeeze out the memory of my embarrassing behavior by scrunching my eyes shut. But it didn't work. It all rushed back to me like a sledgehammer to the head.

I thought Holly was going to *kiss* me. Could I be any more delusional? Why would Holly ever want to kiss me? I mean, that would be like kissing her brother. If she had one. Which she doesn't. But still. What was I *thinking*?

And forget about my vivid imagination, the even worse part was that *I* had almost kissed *her*. If Sarah hadn't screamed when she did, I might have actually gone through with it. So I guess I owed Sarah Saunders one.

Yeah, right.

I held my breath, letting the wave of mortification pass over me. What would Holly have done if my lips had actually met hers? Would she have slapped me? Would she have laughed? Would she have kicked me in the Painful Place? Probably a combination of all three.

"Okay, but it didn't happen," I told myself, climbing out of bed. "It didn't happen and everything's fine and Holly is still your friend."

Even so, the memory kept replaying itself over and over in my head and there was nothing I could do to make it stop. I grabbed my robe and started for the door, hoping a shower would snap me out of it, but I paused when I saw my reflection in the mirror. The eye looked much better this morning and yes, there was a plaid pattern on my forehead, but that would go away. I stared into my eyes and asked myself the question I'd been avoiding asking myself ever since the almost kiss.

"Did you actually want to kiss Holly?" I asked.

The second I said it out loud I got this warm sort of tingly, tight feeling around my heart and I watched my skin flush right in front of me. That would seem to indicate a yes. But what warm-blooded American guy wouldn't have wanted to kiss Holly Stevenson last night? She'd looked downright hot. And besides, we were at a dance, there was all that atmosphere going on. I'd been sucked in, that was all. I'd simply fallen victim to dim lights, slow music, heady perfume, and raging hormones.

Holly was my friend. My best friend. And I wasn't about to do anything to jeopardize that.

I took a deep breath and decided to hit the shower. After all, I did have a long day ahead of me. Last night Dirk had come up with the ultimate plan to expose Scooby for what he really was. That afternoon Rudy and I would put the plan into action. Today Scooby was going to get his. And nothing was going to stand in my way.

I peeked out the window of the Santa Shack, feeling like a fugitive from justice. Or a cat burglar. Or generally like someone who was doing something they shouldn't be doing, which was exactly what I was doing. My mother walked by in her reindeer outfit, heading for the escalator to the food court, and seeing her only magnified the feeling. I glanced at the deserted North Pole. Scooby had gone on his dinner break, but I was sure that at any second, one of the elves was going to come back and catch us here and I'd be shunned like Rudolph from the reindeer games.

"You sure this is going to work?" I asked Rudy, glancing up at him over my shoulder. He was standing on a small stool in the corner, so he was even taller than he usually was.

"Sure, I'm sure," Rudy said. He whipped a tiny screwdriver out of his pocket and used it to tighten the microscopic minicamera into place above the eaves of the Santa Shack. He was cool as a kumquat.

"Why are you so calm?" I asked. Somehow his chill attitude made me intensely nervous. A little stream of sweat ran down from my temple along the side of my face.

Rudy grinned down at me. "I'm just that good," he said, waggling his eyebrows. He jumped down from the stool he was standing on and clapped. "All set. Let's go watch the action."

Rudy walked out of the Santa Shack without even trying to skulk. If anyone caught him, we'd both be subjected to another marathon interrogation in the mall offices, but this fact didn't seem to bother Rudy, perhaps because he knew everyone who worked in this mall and they all seemed to worship the ground he walked on. Apparently in the six months that Rudy had been working at Radio Shack, he'd managed not only to introduce himself to the hundreds of clerks, custodians, and managers, but also to endear himself to them to the point where they all looked on him like a son. Or a brother. Or a really cool cousin.

"So we're going to Sears?" I asked, my nerves calming more and more the farther we got from the North Pole without being accosted.

"That's where I told everyone to meet us," Rudy replied, nodding quickly. "It'll be on, like, fifty screens!"

The mall was packed and Rudy was a fast walker, so I had to dodge and weave to keep up with him. I couldn't wait until Scooby came back from break. This was going to be so perfect. And I owed it all to Rudy and his total AV geek status. We'd spent most of the afternoon planting remote receivers in Radio Shack, in the Sears appliance section, and in the Macy's Juniors section, where TVs suspended over the clothing racks play cheesy pop videos 24/7. We'd even hooked one up behind the big screen in the back of the Disney Store. (The manager has a massive crush on Rudy and was easily convinced to let him "backstage." Yeah. They call their stockroom "backstage." Overcompensating much? News flash: You work in a *mall*!)

"This is gonna be so cool!" Rudy exclaimed as we crossed the threshold into Sears. "We are on a roll, baby! A *roll*!" He jumped on the escalator and took the steps two at a time. I ran after him and suggested he might want to take it down a couple of notches. We didn't want anyone getting suspicious and it wasn't so often that teenage guys were that excited to be hanging out at Sears.

"Good point, man," Rudy said, slapping my chest as he looked around conspiratorially. "Good point."

We walked inconspicuously over to the TV section, where Holly, Flora, Dirk, and Ralph stood waiting. My heart did a weird catch-skip thing the second I saw Holly and when she smiled at me, I quickly looked away. But not before I noticed she was wearing this green turtleneck that made her eyes go like . . . *boom!* Green! Anyway, if she saw the expression on my face, she would know something was up and would grill me endlessly until I told her what it was.

And Holly would never, ever know that I considered kissing her last night. Never, ever.

"Everything set?" Dirk asked, punctuating his question with a twitch. He had a black leather jacket on that made him look not unlike one of those skeezy guys from *Grease*. But still cool, of course.

"Good to go!" Rudy stage-whispered. He glanced at his digital watch. "The fox should be in the hole in less than two minutes."

Ralph nodded and pulled a Twinkie out of his pocket, then proceeded to shove the whole thing into his mouth. Flora watched him in a sort of disgusted awe and he pulled out another Twinkie and held it out to her. She scoffed and looked away, so Ralph offered it to me, but I waved it off. I couldn't even think about eating.

My heart was racing like a reindeer team on too much hot chocolate. If this actually worked, if we actually pulled it off, I was finally, *finally* going to get to see Scooby humiliated! I stared at the big screen in front of us, watching some Michigan running back celebrate a touchdown and waiting for Rudy to hit the button that would switch the feed over to the Santa Shack.

Come on, I thought, glancing at my watch and willing time to move faster. *Come on already!*

"Hey, Nicholas," Holly said casually, stepping around Ralph to stand by my side.

The muscles in my neck instantly tensed up. "Hey," I said, barely looking at her. Couldn't she see I was holding my breath in anticipation here? She was supposed to know me better than anyone.

"So . . . last night was fun," she said, rocking back and forth from her heels to her toes.

Rudy switched the feed over. Every TV in the place was now showing the empty Santa Shack.

"Yeah . . . definitely," I said. I think. I was pretty distracted at this point.

"Listen, do you think we could, like, talk later or something?" Holly asked.

The door of the Santa Shack was opening. "Because I really think we need to—"

"Shhhhhhh!" I shushed her. Loudly. "I want to see this."

Scooby was pulling off his T-shirt.

"I know, but Paul, last night we—"

"Holly! Can you just back off for five seconds?" I snapped. "I'm finally going to get Scooby!"

I threw both arms out toward the screen and all of our friends' heads swiveled around to look at Holly. There were a few moments of silence as Holly turned bright, bright red. My heart was in my stomach, but then Holly turned to look at the television.

"Well, there you go, Paul," she said. She lifted a hand, then let it slap back against her thigh. "Just what you wanted."

I tore my eyes away from her and there, on the screen, was my good friend Scooby, wearing nothing but a pair of fire-engine-red boxers, flexing his non-existent biceps. He turned to check himself out from behind and Rudy and Dirk doubled over laughing. Printed on the back of his boxers was a picture of a muffin with little steam clouds rising off it and the words *Stud Muffin* scrolling over the top.

I had to cover my mouth to keep from laughing out loud. It was even better than I had imagined. Shoppers started to gather around the dozens of television sets, pointing, laughing, glancing around confused. Scooby looked over his shoulder into the mirror and clenched one butt cheek, then the other, then the other, then the other, smiling and nodding in appreciation of himself.

"Aw, yeah!" Rudy said, lifting his hand to slap mine. I put out my hand and he whacked me so hard it stung. I could just imagine the reactions in the

Macy's Juniors section right now and the little kids watching Scooby in the Disney Store. They were going to be scarred for life!

Hmmm . . . maybe we should have thought of that. But whatever. I decided not to dwell on it and to revel in our success instead.

"Gotta hand it to you, Dirk," I said, reaching out to squeeze his shoulder. "This was one hell of a brainstorm."

"Don't touch the leather!" Dirk blurted out. He slipped away from me and let out a violent twitch.

"Okay, okay!" Holly said as Scooby started to wiggle his butt in the mirror and Rudy laughed so hard he had to grab the TV for support. "Have you had enough? Are you done torturing this guy now?"

"What?" I said. "Are you kidding? Not by a long shot!"

"God, Paul, what is wrong with you?" she demanded, stepping in front of the TV and blocking my view.

"What's wrong with me?" I replied, totally confused. "What's wrong with *you*?"

Holly looked at each of our expectant faces as if she was trying to decide whether or not to say what she had to say in front of the assembled parties. "What's *wrong* with me is that you're not working against Christmas here, Paul," she said finally, keeping her stance in front of the television. "All you care about is getting to Scooby."

I lifted my shoulders. "And?"

"*And* it's pathetic!" she replied. Was it just me, or were there suddenly tears in her eyes? "It's perfectly clear that the only reason you're doing any of this is because you're still hung up on Sarah! You're not anti-Christmas, you just can't accept the fact that you got dumped!"

"Hey—"

"No! Forget it!" She looked around at the group again. "I don't know about the rest of you, but I've had it with the anti-Scooby campaign. I'm done helping you try to embarrass this guy."

On TV, Melissa Maya burst into the Santa Shack and started looking around frantically, shoving the half-naked Scooby out of the way. Apparently someone had tipped off mall management. She threw Scooby's costume at him and he quickly wriggled into it. I couldn't help it. I laughed again.

But I stopped when Holly let out a strangled sort of groan.

"You know what else, Nicholas?" she said, suddenly getting right in my face. "I'm also done with *you.*"

Before I could even stifle my grin, Holly had turned on her heel, whipping me in the eye with her hair, and stalked toward the escalator.

Ralph whistled quietly.

"What just happened here?" I asked, totally baffled.

Rudy laughed and slapped me on the shoulder, hitting his remote at the same time to switch all the TVs back to the Michigan game. "She smoked you, my man!"

That night I showed up in Wooddale with my wool hat pulled tightly down over my ears and two scarves wrapped around my neck. It was the coldest night of the year so far, but that hadn't stopped any of the residents from coming out to see their parade. Their pride and joy. Bundled into various coat/hat/mitten/ski mask/earmuff/glove/scarf combinations, people were lined up three rows thick along the sidewalk, breathing into their hands and wrapping their arms around one another for warmth. I saw more than a few thermoses being passed along and heard more than a few jolly laughs. To these people, watching this parade made any degree of frostbite worthwhile.

I used to be one of them.

I joined my friends on the corner in front of Starbucks, where Ralph had staked his claim after leaving the mall. He'd sat outside for a few hours, by himself, in this cold, reading comic books and drinking coffee.

When I walked up, Ralph was surrounded by Dirk, Rudy, and Flora. He had a wild look in his eyes.

"There are cops everywhere, dude. *Everywhere!*" he said, swiveling from side to side and taking up quite a large circumference. "They're on to us, I'm telling you. They know."

"Would you shut up, Ralphie?" Dirk said through his teeth. "You keep spouting off and they *will* be on to us." Dirk, of course, still had on nothing but a T-shirt and his leather jacket and didn't look the least bit cold.

"What's with Ralph?" I asked Flora, who was sipping a cappuccino, cupping it with both hands.

"Too much caffeine makes him paranoid," she answered matter-of-factly. "You should see him after he's had two raspberry iced tea Snapples."

"Ah," I said, glancing around at the people in our immediate vicinity. I leaned back to crane my neck and get a better view into the coffee shop, but no one in there looked familiar.

"Looking for Holly?" Flora asked, raising her tiny eyebrows at me.

"No," I lied.

"She's not coming," Flora said as if I hadn't responded. She looked across the street at a couple of red-faced kids. "She called me a little while ago."

"She called *you*?" I blurted out before I could double-think it.

"And she did not sound happy," Flora said, her voice thick with it's-all-because-of-you meaning.

I felt every muscle in my body coil, but I turned away and took a deep breath to keep from snapping. Who was this girl to tell me how my best friend sounded? Flora knew nothing about Holly and what her various vocal tones meant. And we'd only met these people this week! Now all of a sudden Holly was calling *them* to relay her plans? Why hadn't she called *me*?

Of course I knew why. I'd yelled at her in the middle of the mall. Girls hated that. But this was where I got confused. Holly wasn't a normal girl. We've had plenty of public arguments in our lives and it had never bothered her before. And when it came right down to it, today she'd yelled at me a lot more than I'd yelled at her. *I* was the one who should be angry. Yet she was bothered enough to miss the sabotage of the Wooddale parade? Here I thought I was going to get my chance to apologize and she hadn't even shown up.

"Shhh! You guys! Shhh!" Rudy said, swallowing the ever-present laugh. "Something's going on down there!"

Sure enough, most of the crowd was turning toward the park across the street, mumbling and grumbling to one another. After all, the parade was supposed to have started fifteen minutes ago and the people of Wooddale weren't accustomed to being made to wait. A chunky man in a long overcoat climbed the steps to the platform set up at the edge of the park and tapped the microphone a few times, sending a loud screech of feedback across the town.

Dirk looked at me and grinned maniacally. This was it.

The chunky man took a deep breath and lowered his head. I could tell he was wishing he could be anywhere but here. As I looked down at the expectant faces of the kids around me, I kind of understood the feeling. Maybe disappointing half the populace of Bergen County wasn't the best idea. After all, those kids hadn't done anything wrong—it was Christmas we were out to destroy.

"Hello, everyone, and thank you for coming," he said. "I'm Richard Lembeck, chief of the Wooddale police."

A few clueless people who couldn't feel the palpable foreboding in the air applauded for the man, thinking he was about to kick off the parade.

"I'm sorry to report that due to some technical difficulties, we will not be able to put on the parade this evening," he continued.

An almost-in-unison "Oh no!" went up from the thousands of people lining the street and I suddenly had the feeling I was in Whoville. A heavy pit formed and hardened in the bottom of my stomach. Behind me, Rudy and Dirk exchanged quiet hand slaps and Flora let out a giggle.

"Keep an eye on the town bulletin board, as we may be able to reschedule," Lembeck continued. "Again, thank you for coming." Another screech of feedback and the hiss of the speakers was cut dead. Lembeck beat a hasty retreat to the police van set up on a closed-off street nearby.

The crowd groaned and immediately started to disperse. As anti-Christmas as I'd been feeling lately, the disappointment of the hordes of people around me couldn't be ignored. It had all seemed like harmless fun the other night, but now I was starting to wonder what we'd been thinking.

I was about to voice this thought when I noticed my friends smiling secretively at one another and patting one another on the back.

They wouldn't understand.

"This sucks," a middle school kid said as he walked by us, kicking at a cup on the ground. "This night totally, totally sucks."

Thinking of Holly sitting at home by herself, plotting ways to kill me, I couldn't help agreeing. This night did totally, *totally* suck.

"All right, this is it. I ain't takin' no crap from nobody," I told myself, rubbing my palms together as I approached the basement door at Dirk's on Sunday afternoon. (Sometimes, when I'm trying to psych myself up, I sound like Sylvester Stallone in *Rocky.*)

I had spent most of the morning on the phone in the den, listening to the pounding, sawing, and shouting going on overhead, dialing and redialing Holly's direct line and her cell phone number. Not only had she not picked up, but the machine in her bedroom wasn't on, and the voice mail on her cell phone had reverted to that scary robot voice that says, "The person you are trying to reach is unavailable. If you wish, please leave a message at the tone."

What the hell was going on?

Finally, in a fit of desperation, I'd called Holly's mother's line, which was strictly *verboten*. Whenever Holly's mom got a call from one of her daughter's friends, she very politely told the mistaken caller that she paid for a private line for her daughter for a reason and that if her daughter had not felt the need to give that number to the caller, then there must have, again, been a reason. This speech was normally followed by a deafening slamming down of the phone. Not that Mrs. Stevenson was bitter or anything.

Understandably, I held my breath as Mrs. Stevenson's line rang, but I got the machine there, too. Happy to at least have the opportunity to speak, I told Mrs. Stevenson that I was very sorry for calling but that I feared some kind of debilitating disease had befallen Holly and I'd just like to know if she was okay.

Hadn't gotten a call back. Unbelievable. Holly had suddenly become a master of the cold shoulder.

But she couldn't avoid me forever. Dirk had called an Anti-Christmas Underground meeting and however much she ignored me during the proceedings, I was going to corner her the second it was over and give her a little piece of my mind.

Okay, and maybe I would also apologize. After all, I *had* snapped at her first.

I knocked on the door and it took Ralph a few minutes to get there. When he did, he simply opened the door, nodded, and walked back to the war room, as Dirk called it. I was so psyched for confrontation that when I entered the war room and saw that Holly wasn't there, I deflated so quickly I instantly felt exhausted. I pulled off my hat and looked down at my feet.

"Yo, man! What's up?" Rudy called out, his leg jiggling like crazy. "We weren't doing anything. We were just sitting here waiting for you."

Dirk shot him a look and a twitch. He picked up a piece of paper from the arm of his chair and casually folded it into the back pocket of his jeans, lifting himself up slightly from his seat.

"Holly's not here," Flora said, turning around on the couch so that she could see me. I stood there, my hat literally in my hands. It was nice how Flora was ever so helpful.

"Is she coming?" I asked, taking a seat across from Flora, next to jittery Rudy.

"Nope," Dirk said. He stretched his arms out across the back of the couch on which he always sat alone and tilted his head—on purpose. "She's gone over to the other side."

Well, that didn't sound too promising.

"What does that mean?" I asked. My jacket made a loud crinkling sound in the silence as I sat back into the couch. I couldn't swallow, let alone breathe. I really didn't like the vibe in the room. Something was going on, but I had no idea what it might be. Ralph's eyes had narrowed to such thin slits I couldn't even see the whites anymore.

"Apparently Holly called Flora here this morning and told her that last night, her mother announced that they were going to Aspen for Christmas," Dirk said, lifting a hand toward Flora. "They left this morning."

My mind started off on a tailspin. Holly hadn't mentioned that she and her mother were thinking of going away. She couldn't have just left. Not without telling me. Could she?

"It was a last-minute decision," Flora told me. "Considering what Holly's dad did to them, Holly's mom doesn't like Christmas much, either. Apparently she thought she could only make it merry again if they got the heck out of Jersey."

"Make it merry again," Dirk said with a scoff. "Like that could ever happen."

"So they're gone?" I asked, hardly able to process all the new info.

"Yep. Even as we speak, they're on a whirlwind skiing vacation in good old Colorado," Dirk continued. On the word *whirlwind* he lifted both hands again and waggled his head a little like he was doing a sarcastic happy dance. Then he twitched.

"I don't believe this," I said.

"Oh, you *better* believe it," Dirk said with another quick twitch. "She's somewhere over Nebraska right now."

Ralph opened a can of Mug root beer with a pop as if to emphasize Dirk's statement. I watched him down half the contents and felt my stomach churn. I was nauseous. Physically nauseous. And suddenly very, very hot. I ripped off my jacket and stood up, pacing in front of the semicircle of couches.

"So Holly's . . . *gone*?" I asked, staring at the blinking lights on the police scanner. Holly. In a whole other state. I couldn't even picture it.

"You all right, man?" Dirk asked. He hardly sounded like he cared.

But the answer was no. I was not all right. Holly had left town—nay, the state—and she hadn't even bothered to tell me! Her mother had snapped out of a two-year-long funk and she hadn't called to say, "Hey! Guess what?" And meanwhile my house had a hole in it, my dad was in traction, and we were in our first ever not-talking fight and she didn't even seem to care! Didn't our friendship mean anything to her?

"Holly doesn't even ski," I said under my breath.

"She did not sound psyched about the trip," Flora said, slumping down in her seat. "She told me she just felt like she had to get out of here."

Again, filled with meaning. This-is-all-because-of-you meaning.

But what had I *done*?

Suddenly, even in the presence of four other anti-Christmas brethren, I felt utterly and completely alone. I'd been deserted by my best friend and there was no way to get her back.

Christmas had just hit a whole new level of awful.

Run, Run, Rudolph

WHEN I WOKE UP ON MONDAY MORNING, MY BLACK eye was almost healed, which meant that soon I would be going back to work as Santa, which meant I was going to have to start hanging out with Scooby again. A lot.

The very thought of being forced to work with him made my skin crawl. After everything that had happened in the past couple of weeks, ending up with Holly deserting me, I felt like someone deserved to pay. Not only that, but I felt like I, just once, deserved to come out on top. But as long as I was forced to be around Scooby, I was the big fat loser.

There was only one logical conclusion—one of us had to go. And it was not going to be me. Scooby was a fake. A creep. A guy who used his position as Santa to sell his crappy CD. So getting him fired wasn't just an act of revenge. It was the right thing to do.

After school on Monday, I drove straight to Dirk's house. (When Mom found out Holly had skipped town, she let me use my dad's car to drive myself to school.) This time I didn't even wait to knock on the door. I tried the knob, it turned, and I walked right into the war room. I was filled with such a sense of purpose, such a seething hatred, that I was completely wound. I had about a million ideas on how to solidify Scooby's fate and they were all bouncing around in my head like pinballs. I needed someone to help me sort it all out.

Dirk, Ralph, Rudy, and Flora were all gathered around the coffee table, looking at a large sheet of paper that was rolled out in front of them. The police scanner crackled away in the corner while Dirk talked in low tones. The others seemed to hang on his every word, nodding periodically. None of them even noticed my manic entrance.

"Everyone!" I announced, clapping and causing Flora and Rudy to jump. "I'm here to tell you I'm done messing around."

Dirk shot Ralph a look and stood up to face me over the couch. Ralph rolled up the large sheet of paper and put it under the table as Rudy and Flora turned in their seats to face me.

"You didn't knock," Dirk said, pressing his fist into his palm. He was wearing a black tank top and his muscles flexed intimidatingly.

"So? I'm one of you now," I said with a shrug. I saw Flora and Ralph exchange a dubious look, but I chose to ignore it. It didn't matter if they were unconvinced of my anti-Christmas dedication. They would be convinced. Very soon.

"Look, I need to get Scooby fired and I need you guys to help me make it happen," I said, walking to the front of the arc of couches. "I have a lot of ideas, but they pretty much all require us to break the law."

Dirk frowned, pondering this, then twitched. "Which law would that be?" he asked, slowly lowering himself onto his personal couch.

I took a deep breath and paused dramatically. (Hey, I'm not immune to a little drama when it's my turn in the spotlight. It doesn't happen very often.) I smiled slowly and looked at each of my friends. Their eyes were trained on me, waiting. I knew they were all intrigued. I could feel it in the air.

"How would you guys feel about hiding out in the mall tonight until after closing?" I asked, raising my eyebrows as I shoved my hands in my pockets.

Flora and Rudy sat back in their seats and turned to look at Dirk. There was a long, might I say *impressed* silence as everyone mulled over my proposed act of juvenile delinquency. Dirk's eyes slid from Ralph over to Flora and Rudy. He leaned forward, rested his elbows on his knees, and folded his hands together under his chin. Then, ever so slowly, he smiled, his brown eyes seeming to darken.

"I think hanging out at the mall until after closing is a fine idea," he said.

I grinned for real now as pride surged through me. The Anti-Christmas Underground had my back. They knew what was important—what really mattered— and they were willing to break the law to help me. Who needed Holly when I had friends like these?

"This is so cool, man! This is so totally, totally cool!" Rudy stage-whispered as we lay on our stomachs on the grimy mall floor on Monday night. When Mom and I went to see my dad earlier that afternoon, I'd told them I was going over to Matt's to watch *Monday Night Football,* so I was covered until at least eleven o'clock. If all went as planned, I'd be home right on time.

Rudy, Dirk, and I were hidden under one of the lower valleys in the snowy hills that made up Santa Land. There was about two inches of space between our heads and the plastic and wood structure above us. With almost all the mall lights extinguished, it was pitch-black under there. If Rudy and Dirk hadn't breathed, smelled, and talked so very differently, I wouldn't have been able to tell who was on either side of me. And, of course, there was the fact that Dirk twitched every few minutes, his leg kicking out to whack me in the ankle. It was definitely leaving a mark.

"Rudy, you brought the pot, right?" Dirk asked, his voice coming from the darkness to my left.

Rudy giggled, earning a "shhh!" from Flora, who was a few feet away with Ralph, sitting under one of the higher hills.

"Yeah, I got the pot," Rudy whispered. He elbowed me in the side and I could hear the rustling of a plastic bag as he pulled it from his pocket. "Rita's gonna kill me when she realizes I took her stash, but it'll all be worth it."

"You better believe it," I told him. "Dirk, you got the vodka?" I asked.

"Hey, who're you talkin' to?" he asked indignantly. "Of course I got the booze."

I grinned in the darkness, happy that no one could see exactly how giddy I was. The Underground had loved most of my plans, but it was agreed that there was only one that was a surefire way to get Scooby fired. No one would want an alcoholic druggie listening to their kids' Christmas wishes, so that was what we were turning Scooby into—a classic teenage burnout.

I'd taken one of my extra Santa suits, which could have belonged to either of us, and splashed enough alcohol over it to make it reek. Rudy had lifted a dime bag of pot from his aunt Rita's closet and Dirk had swiped a bottle of vodka from his dad's hidden stash in the garage. Once we were sure the coast was clear, we were going to sneak into the Santa Shack, plant all three offending items in Scooby's locker, and leave an anonymous message on Papadopoulos's voice mail, tipping him off.

For a moment I found myself wishing Holly were there to witness my ultimate triumph, but in truth she probably wouldn't have even shown. If she thought the whole live broadcast from the Santa Shack was too much, she definitely wouldn't be down with this plan.

"You guys, how long do we have to stay here?" Flora's voice came from the blackness. "I think Ralph's about to have a panic attack."

As if to illustrate her point, a high-pitched whimper sounded from the corner.

"He's claustrophobic," Rudy explained.

"Well, I think we're pretty safe," I said, reaching down to grab the Santa suit. "We've been in here for over an hour."

I started to shimmy out of my hiding place, but I felt a strong hand on my left shoulder. "Hold on, Paulie," Dirk said. "We have a new plan."

"Dirk!" Flora whispered. "I thought we decided not to tell him!"

"Well, I changed my mind," Dirk shot back.

My heart started to beat with a fear/excitement cocktail. This sounded interesting. Dangerous. But somehow I knew that whatever Dirk had come up with to bring Scooby down had to be ten times better than my plan. He was an anti-Christmas genius.

"Flora, is there room for us over there?" Dirk asked, sliding away from me and moving in Ralph and Flora's direction.

"Yeah, I think so," came the exasperated-sounding response.

"This is gonna be so great!" Rudy said as we both crawled toward the more open part of the hills. My back twinged with every movement and I realized exactly how long we'd been waiting in the same position. Oh, the things I'd do to get to Scooby!

I felt the roof open a bit above my head and suddenly a flashlight flicked on. My heart got caught in my already constricted throat. But then I saw that Ralph was holding the light and I started to breathe again. Ralph sat with his back pressed up against the inside wall of the hill, dwarfing Flora, who sat next to him, her knee pressed against his. Dirk crawled into position next to Flora, and Rudy and I joined them, forming a very tight little circle, almost all our body parts touching.

Shadows cast by the sole light danced across my friends' faces, making them look almost sinister. Everyone seemed to be watching me and sizing me up as if they'd never met me before. Clearly no one was sure how I was going to react to this new plan. It only made me salivate to hear it.

"Ralph," Dirk said, never taking his eyes off me. "The plans."

Ralph pulled out a large sheet of paper from behind him and unfolded it across all of our legs. I realized it was the same sheet they had been poring over earlier that afternoon when I'd surprised them in the war room. I studied all the lines and numbers and boxes and arrows, and it took me a couple of minutes to realize I was looking at a blueprint of the mall.

Wow. These people were organized.

When I looked up at Dirk, waiting to hear about the new plan, they were all still gazing at me. Suddenly I felt like I'd missed something. My heart slamming against my rib cage, I looked down at the blueprint again. That was when I noticed the words, written in neat block letters, across the top of the page near Sears.

Operation Mall Meltdown.

I looked at Dirk again.

"So?" I said. "What's the plan? What's Operation Mall Meltdown?"

"My friend," Dirk said, reaching out and slapping a hand down on my shoulder. He gave it a little squeeze. "We are going to burn this mall to the ground."

There was a moment of charged silence. And then I laughed.

"You're funny," I said. "What's the real plan?"

"That *is* the plan," Flora said, rolling her eyes. "We're burning down the mall."

"Isn't it so cool?" Rudy blurted out, grinning.

I gave myself a moment to wake up from the

nightmare. When that didn't happen, I started to panic. It must have been written all over my face because Flora closed her eyes and tipped back her head.

"I told you he wouldn't go for it," she said. "We should have just left the goody-goody at home."

"You can't do this," I said, looking at Dirk. "Do you realize what's gonna happen if you get caught?"

"*We* are not gonna get caught," Dirk said confidently.

"Come on, man," Rudy said, nudging me with his knee. "We're gonna make history tonight."

I looked from face to shadow-blocked face and a cold, sick realization seeped through me. These people were freakin' maniacs! I was mashed into a crawl space with a bunch of total lunatics!

Dirk started to roll up the plans and I suddenly knew what I had to do—grab the blueprint and run. I was closest to the little opening we'd used to get in here. If I snatched the paper, it would take them a couple of seconds to get over the shock, which would give me a good head start. All this contemplation took about half a second and I was just reaching out to grab the plans when I heard a door slam. Very nearby.

Everyone froze. I could actually feel Dirk's and Rudy's muscles tense up. Ralph fumbled and then cut the light and we were plunged into complete darkness again.

Voices. Muffled but close. My hands clenched into fists. Someone had seen our light or heard our voices. We were going to get caught. And I was going to get sent down the river with the rest of the loonies.

"Who the hell is still here?" Dirk whispered.

I listened to the footsteps, trying to discern how

many people were out there. They were moving very slowly and I squeezed my eyes shut, willing them to just keep going. If they were late workers, maybe they would just leave. But after a few minutes that felt like days, I couldn't take the waiting. Every second, it sounded like the voices were getting closer. If they were going to find us, I wished they'd just get it over with already.

"I'm gonna go look," I whispered finally.

"No!" Flora's voice protested.

I didn't listen. I hit my stomach and crawled back toward the opening, using my elbows and hands to move along. As I went, a thousand thoughts fought it out in my brain. If it was mall security, maybe I could flag them down and turn the others in. Maybe Dale Dombrowski would believe me if I told him I was tricked into the plot. Then, at least, the mall wouldn't be burned down. But could I do it? Could I really turn these people in? And what if Dale *didn't* believe me?

Oh God. I was going to jail. A hot, acidy dread seared through my stomach as I came to the opening at the edge of the fake hills. I was going to jail and my parents were going to kill me, not necessarily in that order. Why had I ever gotten involved in this? Why? *Why?*

I moved aside the white sheet that camouflaged the opening and peeked out ever so slowly. The first thing I saw made my blood boil so fast I started to sweat.

Scooby. He was the answer. He was the reason I had gotten myself into this mess. And he was standing less than five feet away. But that wasn't even the kicker. The person he was talking to was none other than That Awful Woman. Marge Horvath herself.

My first instinct was to hurl myself out of my

hiding space and tackle them both to the ground, using the element of surprise to pummel them as much as possible before they overpowered me. But as I watched them, my anger started to subside into suspicious curiosity. What were these two doing in the mall after hours, talking intently to each other, their heads bent close together? What could a talent-less teenage rap artist and a vindictive, pinched jew-elry store manager have in common?

As I watched, the pair started to move across the mall toward one of the exits. Part of me was itching to follow. But my survival instinct pulled my eyes toward the other exit—the one on the opposite side of the mall. The one that I could use to escape from the head cases hiding behind me. With any luck I could make it to my dad's car and call the police from my cell while simultaneously slamming on the gas and peeling the heck out of here. I held my breath. It was time to make a break for it.

I put one hand outside the opening and then heard Marge's voice carry across the empty mall, echo-ing against the walls, as clear as a bell.

"I still can't believe they blamed the whole thing on that Nicholas woman," she said, causing my blood to instantly run cold. "Like she possesses the imagina-tion to pull something like that off."

They laughed, both of them, and my mind reeled. Blamed what on my mother? She couldn't be talking about the money skimming, could she? Marge *knew* my mother didn't do it and she hadn't said anything?

"Her son's a moron, too," Scooby said. "Must be in the blood."

My jaw clenched in anger and suddenly I forgot about Operation Mall Meltdown. I forgot about the rest of the Anti-Christmas Underground, sitting a few feet back through the tunnel, plotting arson. I glanced at the door to freedom and made a snap decision. If Marge knew something that could clear my mother's name, I was going to find out what it was. And maybe I really would tackle Scooby to the ground and kick his butt—if the opportunity presented itself.

As soon as Scooby's and Marge's backs were to me, I slipped out of the crawl space and flattened myself up against the nearest support beam in the center of the mall, the *Mission Impossible* music playing in my head. The sheet over the opening moved and Dirk stuck his head out.

"What are you doing?" he whispered.

I shook my head and lifted a finger to my lips, casting my eyes in Scooby and Marge's direction. Dirk saw them and we locked eyes for a moment before he disappeared again. I knew he thought I would signal them when the coast was clear, but that wasn't my plan. My plan was to follow Scooby and Marge wherever they went and find out what was going on between my archnemesis and my mother's.

Marge and Scooby walked through the inner doors of the exit by the courtesy counter and I stepped out from my hiding place to follow.

"Hey!" someone shouted, his voice filling the entire deserted mall. "Don't you take another step, young man."

I stopped, my foot suspended in the air, and my arms instinctively flew up over my head. I couldn't have breathed if I'd tried.

"Okay. Turn around slowly."

I hopped on my one foot awkwardly, afraid to let the other touch the ground, until I had turned around and was facing Dale Dombrowski. He was standing a few feet away from me, legs about two feet apart and bent at the knee, and he was wielding a stun gun.

"Aw, Paul," he said, standing up straight and shaking his head. "I really didn't want to believe it was you."

My heart sank at the disappointment in the man's eyes. What had I done? How had I gotten here?

"You're gonna want to have a seat right there and put your hands on your head," Dale said. "The police are on their way and your friends will be with you shortly."

There was a sudden scuffle and a few loud thumps and I heard Dirk yell, "Don't touch me! Don't touch me, you stinkin' rent-a-cop!"

"All right! Everybody out!" Dale shouted, walking over to the crawl space and lifting the white sheet.

Rudy crawled out first and pushed himself to his feet, hands raised as he looked around wildly. Flora shimmied out after him. She crossed her arms over her chest in irritation. Finally Ralph and Dirk appeared, walking around from the other side of Santa Land, three mall security guys behind them. Dirk shot me a look that could have melted the whole North Pole in seconds.

"Nice to tell me there was another opening on the other side," he said, sitting down next to me. "They ambushed us."

I'd had no idea there was another opening, but I didn't bother saying it. What was the point? We were all snagged and we were all going down and I hadn't even done anything wrong. Well, except hide out in the mall after hours plotting to get someone fired.

One of the younger, pudgier security cops held up Dirk's blueprints. "Dale, you're gonna want to take a look at this," he said.

Ralph hung his head and Flora rolled her eyes, then closed them, leaning back against the support beam. Dirk started to twitch wildly. I glanced at Rudy and I could swear he was starting to cry.

"Very interesting," Dale said as he looked over Operation Mall Meltdown. He turned and gazed at us sadly. "Looks like you kids are in a whole heap o' trouble."

At that moment, just when I thought things couldn't possibly get worse, Scooby and Marge walked in from the parking lot again.

"See, Dale? I told you your stakeout would be worthwhile," Scooby said, smirking. "This kid is, like, stalking me!"

"Between him and his money-skimming mother, they're like a crime *family*," Marge said, laughing at her own lame joke.

Looking as triumphant as could be, Scooby and Marge turned around once again and practically floated out of the mall, their laughter echoing through my head. My heart clenched into the tightest of tight little balls as what Scooby had said sank in. He had called for the rent-a-cop stakeout. If not for his tip, Dale might never have caught us.

"He set us up," Dirk said, glaring at Scooby's retreating back. "The jolly bastard set us up."

I'll Have a Blue, Blue, Blue, Blue Christmas

"THE IMPORTANT THING IS WE GOT OUR MESSAGE OUT there. Tomorrow this is gonna be in all the papers—the *Record*, the *Ridgewood News*, *Community Life*. They might even pick this story up in Rockland or the *Post* or something. Everyone will hear about the Anti-Christmas Underground. They can't ignore us anymore. . . ."

I lifted my head out of my hands and looked over at Dirk. He was sitting on a hard wooden bench, exactly like mine, across the cold gray cell from me. As he rambled, he rocked forward and back, his hands pressed into the bench at his sides, his head twitching every few seconds. Rudy lay on the bench next to me, his arm crooked behind his head, his eyes closed, more still than I'd ever seen him. Flora sat on the floor in the corner, her legs crossed in some yoga pose, her eyes closed in meditation. Ralph sat next to Dirk, playing quite beautifully, actually, on a harmonica. I do not know now, nor will I ever know, where the heck he got it from.

"Nope, they can't ignore us anymore. We've brought our message to the world and now disenfranchised kids like us all over the globe will be validated. They will rise up and join our cause. This is a fine day for our organization, gentlemen. A fine day . . ."

"Dirk!" I shouted, silencing him and surprising everyone in the cell, including myself. "Has the fact that we're in jail right now escaped your attention?"

Dirk stopped rocking and glared at me. "What's your point, Paulie?" he asked, his head twitching so hard I swear I heard a snap.

"My point is, *we're in JAIL!*" I shouted, standing up. "There is no other point. That, in itself, is a pretty large point!"

"Everyone has to make sacrifices for the cause," Dirk said, rising to face me. "It's about time you learned that."

"Yeah? Well, I've already made plenty of sacrifices," I told him, taking a step closer to his short but powerful frame. "I lost my girlfriend, my best friend, my bedroom, and my Jeep. My father's in the hospital and by now I'm sure my mother has had a nervous breakdown, so don't talk to me about sacrifices."

My last words hung in the air and for a moment I thought I'd gotten through to Dirk—that he would back down—but then Flora broke the silence.

"This is all your fault, you know," she said. This seemed to be her favorite sentiment when it came to yours truly. Her feet scraped against the floor as she pushed herself up. "If you hadn't wanted to get back at Scooby so bad, you wouldn't even be here. Holly was right. You're not anti-Christmas, you're anti-Guy Who Stole Your Girlfriend."

"You couldn't be more wrong," I said, stung.

"Oh yeah? Then why were you trying to follow him out of the mall tonight instead of helping us with Operation Mall Meltdown?" Rudy asked, turning his head but otherwise not moving. "I saw you, man. I watched you from the opening. You weren't sticking around. You just wanted to see what that scrawny freak was up to."

I swallowed hard.

"If it wasn't for you and your Scooby obsession, none of us would be here," Flora said. "You never would have crawled out of the hills and we never would have gotten caught. Think about *that*."

She reached up and flicked me on the forehead. She flicked me hard.

"Paul Nicholas?" There was a loud clattering of keys and we all looked over to find Sergeant Pie, our arresting officer, whose face seemed to represent his name, unlocking the cell door.

"Yeah?" I said, happy to have an excuse to take a step away from Flora, who suddenly seemed more dangerous than the rest of them.

"You made bail," Pie said, sliding open the barred door with a clang. "You're free to go."

I glanced at Dirk and Rudy and wiped my palms on my jeans. "Well . . . see ya," I said.

"That's right, traitor," Dirk blurted out. "Go home to your mommy now."

My brain was void of comebacks. I did feel like a traitor, but I couldn't figure out why. These people were out of their minds. I should be glad to be rid of them. But something in what Flora said rang true. If it hadn't been for my selfish act, maybe none of us would have been here. Maybe I could have found another way to stop their little arson plot and we'd all have been sitting at the Suburban right now, laughing over what we'd almost done.

Part of me wanted to apologize, but that didn't seem right, either. So all I did was duck my head and slip through the door, leaving my so-called friends behind. As I walked off, Ralph played the classic theme of humiliated defeat on the harmonica: "Na na na na, na na na na, hey hey hey! Good-bye!"

I followed Pie into the outer office and stopped in my tracks. My mother sat in a battered wooden chair in the corner, her face wet, her skin so pale it conjured images of the Ghost of Christmas Yet to Come. When she saw me, she stood up shakily, gripping my jacket, which they'd taken from me, in both hands.

"Mom," I said, my voice cracking.

She walked over and gave me a quick hug, but when she pulled away, all I could see in her eyes was anger and disappointment. The pain in my chest was excruciating. I don't think I'd ever disappointed my mother in my life. I didn't like it.

"Mom, I—"

"It would be better if you didn't talk right now," she said.

I looked down, ashamed, and glimpsed the edge of a little green envelope sticking out of her pocketbook. She saw my face and quickly shoved the envelope farther into her bag, but not before I realized what it was. Her Christmas gift fund envelope—the place where she kept the money she'd saved all year for gifts.

My mother had used her gift fund to bail me out of jail.

"Let's go," she said, grabbing my arm and nudging me toward the door. She looked at Sergeant Pie and forced a smile. "Thank you, Officer. Merry Christmas."

My heart split in two when she said that. My mom. She never let the spirit die.

The moment we hit the cold night air, something seemed to snap within my mother and all the words she was holding inside came pouring off her tongue.

"I just don't understand it, Paul. I just don't understand it," she said, speed-walking over to the car. "I think you're watching football with your friends and I get a phone call from the police—the *police*—telling me they have you in custody for attempted arson?"

I looked at her over the top of the car and her eyes were so wide she could have been looking at the Abominable Snowman over my shoulder.

"Mom, I—"

"Didn't I tell you not to speak?" she asked.

My mouth snapped shut and we both got in the car.

"Known hoodlums!" she exclaimed as she started the engine. "You've been consorting with known hoodlums! Do you know that Officer Pie told me that all of those kids you were caught with have rap sheets as long as an AK-47—which they probably keep under their beds?"

Even in the insanity I almost laughed.

"Is something funny, Paul?" she snapped, her hand on the gearshift.

"No, Mom," I said. "I swear I didn't know they—"

"I don't want to hear it," she told me, shaking her head. "I just want to drive home in peace."

My mother pulled the car out into traffic, taking

long, deep, steady breaths. I was dying to ask her what, exactly, my "friends" had on their rap sheets, but at this point I definitely knew better than to try to talk. I looked out the window at the decorated houses flying by and sank down in my seat.

This was it. This was the moment I hit rock bottom.

I had no idea what was going to happen next, but I was definitely going to get fired from the mall. And losing my job was going to make it a lot harder to bring Scooby down.

The second this thought crossed my mind, I felt sick to my stomach. Bringing Scooby down? Was that all I could think about? Was that what really mattered to me? I mean, come on! What was destroying Scooby really going to accomplish?

Would it make Sarah come back to me? Probably not. Would it make Holly come home? Definitely not. Would it get my mother her job back, get my father out of the hospital, or restore my room?

No, no, and no.

Here I'd been focusing all my time and energy on getting back at Scooby and where had it gotten me? Nowhere. Oh, besides *jail.*

My mother turned onto our block and pulled the car to a stop in front of our house, where a huge industrial waste bin stood on the lawn, full of roofing and jagged boards. I looked up at my dark, undecorated, lonely old house and sighed.

This was, without a doubt, the worst Christmas ever.

My mother got out of the car and stalked inside. I followed as slowly as possible, anticipating another reaming, but when I closed the door behind me, I heard her banging around in the kitchen. I stopped with my hand on the doorknob, feeling like someone had taken a spoon and hollowed me out.

When the Christmas tree is up, my mother always, *always,* without fail, walks right into the living room and plugs it in whenever we return to the house. Always. The fact that she was in the kitchen at that moment and the tree was still dark brought home exactly how much I had hurt her.

I stood at the open entryway and watched her make herself some hot chocolate. I was trying to think of something to say. Something that would make my mother feel better. That was when I remembered what Marge had said earlier in the evening. It was a long shot, but maybe . . .

"Hey, Mom, I don't think Marge thinks you took that money from the store," I blurted out.

My mother paused. "What do you mean?" she asked, her back facing me as she braced her hands on the counter.

"Just that . . ." And then I realized that there was nothing to what Marge had said. All she'd done was tell Scooby she thought my mother was too stupid to skim money from the registers.

"Just that I think she thinks you're innocent," I concluded lamely. So much for making her feel better. Nice one, Paul.

"Well, it's nice to know someone does, even if it is That Awful Woman," my mother said, turning to face me. "But let's get back to the subject at hand. I'm not going to tell your father about this. Not yet. I'm afraid it might make him worse."

"Mom, I know you don't want me to talk, but I just want to say that I really am sorry," I told her.

She took a deep breath and let it out slowly through her nose, facing the counter again. "I know you are, Paul," she said, turning so that I could see her profile. "But I think that right now you should just go to your room."

"I . . . I can't," I told her. "My room is—"

"Finished!" she said with false brightness. She turned completely around now and braced her hands behind her on the counter. "I was going to surprise you when you got home tonight. They finished your room this afternoon."

My throat swelled up with emotion. There was no way I could speak.

"Merry Christmas," my mother said flatly. Then she turned away from me again. "We'll talk about all this in the morning."

Slowly I walked over to the stairs. I could see from where I was standing that she'd tied a huge red bow on my bedroom door. I didn't know exactly what was inside, but if I knew my mother at all, I could bet she'd had a new bed delivered and had spent half the day at Bed, Bath & Beyond picking out sheets and pillows. She'd probably worked on the place for hours while I was plotting to break the law—and her heart.

I climbed the stairs, each step feeling heavy enough to shake the house, and walked over to my room, but I couldn't do it. I couldn't open the door and have it thrown right in my face—what a great mom I had and what a bad son I was.

Next to my bedroom door there's a niche in the

wall to display figurines or photographs. Every day during the Christmas season my mom puts little treats there so that if I get hungry while studying or if I have friends over, there's always something to eat. Today, standing in the little indentation was a statue of Santa Claus, made out of Rice Krispies treats. His little arm was raised in a wave, and his mouth was drawn up like a bow, just like in "'Twas the Night Before Christmas."

Before I could even breathe, I was overcome with a violent rage. I braced my hands on the wall above the indentation and glared down at Santa.

"I hate you," I said through my teeth. "I lost my Santa hat and you turned against me. You turned all of Christmas against me. If it wasn't for you, none of this would have happened!"

I grabbed Santa, ripped off his head, and stuffed it into my mouth.

"You're going to pay for what you've done to me," I said through my sticky teeth. "You are going to pay!"

Jolly Old Saint Nicholas

"What the heck was that?" I whispered into the darkness of my bedroom, clutching my new sheets to my sides. Something had jolted me awake. A noise? A movement? What? My heart was pounding in my chest, and, like a little kid who's just had a nightmare, I was afraid to even look left or right. If there was something freaky in my room, maybe it wouldn't see me if I didn't see *it*.

A couple of minutes of holding my breath and I started to relax. A few very weak, very pink rays of sunlight were starting to peek through my windows. Maybe it was nothing. Just part of a nightmare I could no longer recall. I was just letting my heavy eyelids close again when I heard it.

It was faint at first, so faint I thought I might already be dreaming. But it gradually grew louder and louder. A persistent jolly tinkling sound. The sound of jingling bells.

I sat up straight in bed. Okay, now I was sure I

was losing it. Who would be outside jingling bells at five o'clock in the morning?

I whipped off my blankets and swung my legs over the side of the bed. Moving the stiff new curtains aside ever so slightly so that the psycho outside wouldn't notice, I looked out.

That was when I *knew* I was still sleeping. Because there was no way I was seeing what I thought I was.

"Ho ho ho!" the freak on the lawn shouted, waving a velvet-gloved hand at me. "Merry Christmas, Paul!"

It knew my name! The freak knew my name!

I turned away from the window, grabbed my robe, and flew down the stairs. "I am not going insane, I am not going insane, I am not going insane," I chanted as I pushed my arms into the sleeves. I was going to get outside, the wind was going to knock me out of my sleepwalking stupor, and I was going to wake up to a normal day. Or as normal as the day could be when I'd been arrested the night before.

I flung open the front door and my heart literally stopped for half a second.

My whole house was ablaze with Christmas lights. They dripped from the eaves and surrounded the windows and doors. They laced the bushes that lined the house and ran along the ground on either side of the front walk. My father's Santa in Space extravaganza was in full effect, except the iridescent space-ship was set up on the front lawn instead of the roof. And the Santa inside it was not plastic. The Santa inside it was *real*.

"Hello, Paul," Santa said with a twinkle in his deep blue eyes. Then the spaceship let out a huge burst of dry-ice steam from its rocket blasters. Just like my father had planned.

"Uh . . . hi?" I said, my arms hanging limp at my sides as Santa stepped out of the ship.

He smiled and patted his stomach as he gazed at me. "The answer to your question is yes, Paul. It really is me. It's Santa Claus. I'm the real thing."

My head started to pound as I looked into his eyes, trying to find the truth, but it didn't take long. As I looked at him, a sudden, soothing, even elating warmth came over me and my heart tingled with anticipation just like it did every Christmas Eve. It was true. I was standing on my front lawn in my pajamas with Kris Kringle himself.

"Wow," I said under my breath. "Wow."

"Paul," Santa said, his eyes suddenly narrowing a bit but never losing their twinkle. "We have to talk."

He brought his big hand down on my shoulder and turned me around. We walked together over to the front steps and Santa sat down. As I stood there, unsure of what to do, he reached into his sleeve and pulled out a candy cane.

"Peppermint?" he asked, offering it to me.

"No thanks," I said as I dropped down next to him.

I have to say, I couldn't stop staring. It isn't every day a person gets to meet the real Santa. His thick red suit stretched over his sizable belly and was fastened up the front with silver buttons, each in the shape of a different snowflake. The white fur around his collar and the edges of his sleeves had wisps of light brown in it and his black boots were cracked and mud caked, the laces fraying. I guess getting in and out of a sled a billion times over will do that to your footwear.

"Mama always shines them up for me on Christmas Eve," Santa said, picking up his left foot slightly when he noticed me looking. "They're a bit well worn right now, I'm afraid."

"I can't believe you're actually here," I said, inhaling the pure evergreen scent that surrounded him and trying to commit it to memory.

"Well, son, you brought me here," Santa said. He stroked his beard—real curly whiskers as pure white as new-fallen snow—and looked down at his lap for a moment. "You know, I've always admired you and your family, Paul," he said, looking me in the eye again. "The Nicholas clan has always understood the true spirit of Christmas. You live it all year round. Do you have any idea how rare that is in this day and age?"

I felt a cold sliver of guilt start to slice its way through my gut. "Yeah," I replied, because I felt I had to.

"Well, gosh darn it, Paul, you've really gone and messed it up this year, haven't you?" Santa chided.

I blinked at him. "How did you—"

"You forget, Paul. I know everything," Santa said, leaning toward me slightly. "But to be sure, I never thought I'd see the day when Paul Nicholas of Paramus, New Jersey, U.S.A., would wind up on my naughty list." He shook his head and looked away with a sad sigh.

I couldn't believe it. I'd disappointed Santa. What was the world coming to?

"I'm sorry, Santa," I said, staring down at my plaid flannel pajama pants. "It's just, I lost my Santa hat and then everything started to fall apart. My girlfriend broke up with me, my dad was electrocuted, my house burned down, and now my best friend has up and left me. I thought . . . well . . . I guess I thought Christmas was punishing me," I finished lamely.

"None of this has anything to do with your Santa hat. Can't you see that yet, Paul?" Santa asked me, placing his hands on his knees. "Your father and the house . . . well . . . that was an accident. But everything else you've told me was your own doing. You can't blame Christmas because you chose the wrong girl."

Huh? my brain asked. "The wrong girl?" I said.

"Don't you see, Paul? Sarah wasn't the girl for you. She never had the true spirit of Christmas," Santa explained. "All Sarah Saunders cares about is Sarah Saunders. And presents. Trust me, I know. I've been getting her Christmas list for the past sixteen years. Last year it was so big she sent it to me on a Zip disk. I don't even know what a Zip disk is."

Santa chuckled and I did, too. That sounded like Sarah.

"You're better off without her," Santa said, patting me on the back and sending another shot of warmth right through me. "Look what she's done to you. You ended up torturing that Scooby kid, yelling at your best friend, falling in with a bunch of anti-Christmas hooligans. Paul, you sabotaged the Wooddale parade!"

My head fell into my hands. The last thing a guy like me ever wanted to hear was Santa Claus's voice listing my many, many mistakes.

"Oh, son, I didn't come here to make you feel bad," Santa said, reaching out to tousle my hair. "I came here to tell you it's not too late. You can still save Christmas."

"But . . . but how?" I asked, lifting my head.

"Well, you know the true spirit of Christmas is making the people you love happy," Santa said, his eyes twinkling like stars.

"Right," I said. "But how am I supposed to do that now? My mom hates me, my dad's in the hospital, and I don't even know *where* Holly is." Just saying it made me feel suddenly and irrevocably overwhelmed, like a cold boulder was pressing down on my chest.

"You miss her, don't you?" Santa asked, his voice a kind, soothing rumble.

The moment he said it, I felt like my heart was going to curl up and die. I'd been trying not to think about it—focusing on Scooby and all that—but I missed Holly so much it actually hurt. I saw her in my mind, standing in front of me at the Holiday Ball, her eyes at half-mast, and suddenly I saw myself kissing her. Felt myself kissing her. My whole body flushed. And I realized. I should have done it. I *wanted* to do it. I wanted to kiss Holly Stevenson. And I wanted her to want to kiss me back.

"Shoulda gone for it, son," Santa said, slapping my back.

I almost choked.

"But it's not too late," he answered. "Holly's the *right* girl. And just realizing that is half the battle."

"But I don't even know where she is!" I told him, my voice embarrassingly high-pitched. "And I still have to fix everything else! What am I supposed to do here, Santa?"

"Ho ho ho," Santa laughed quietly. "Take it easy there, Paul. All you have to do is take it one problem at a time."

"One problem at a time," I repeated.

Santa smiled slowly, knowingly. "The answers are right in front of you, Paul," he said, rising from the step. He turned to stand right in front of me and laid his hands over his stomach. "You can't trust every guy in a Santa suit."

I opened my mouth to ask him what he meant, but Santa simply winked and in a sudden whirl of magical snow, he was gone.

I woke up with a start and looked around my room like a madman. Sunlight streamed through my windows and the red numbers on my digital clock read 7:15. My heart filled with disappointment. Was it all just a dream?

I jumped out of bed, ran downstairs, and whipped open the front door. The front yard was as barren and dull as it had been the day before. There were no lights on my house, no sign that anything had happened. As I stood there on the front steps, where Santa and I had supposedly sat just a couple of hours ago, I felt my shoulders start to slump. The mind really could play some evil tricks. How could I have ever let myself think that it was real?

I trudged back up to my room, pondering the chances of my mother letting me stay home from school, but the second I got back to my doorway, I froze. Every inch of my skin tingled and suddenly, I could smell that evergreen scent that had filled my senses when I was chatting with Santa.

There, sitting on my pillow, was a Santa hat. I flung myself onto the bed, grabbed the hat, and turned it inside out. My name, in my own crappy handwriting, was scrawled across the brim. The semimatted fur. The cocoa stain. I lifted the hat to my face, closed my eyes, and inhaled. Ahhh . . . mulberry wine!

It wasn't just any Santa hat. It was *my* Santa hat. And there was only one way it could have gotten there, only one person who could have pulled off such an amazing Christmas miracle. The big guy. Santa himself. I pulled the hat on over my head and savored the warmth that rushed over me.

Maybe Christmas hadn't forsaken me after all.

You're a Mean One,
Mr. Grinch

Sometimes, when I'm hyper or excited or inspired or just happy, my brain seems to function on two levels. I can do two things at once—like programming the VCR while vacuuming (my weekly chore that I manage to do once a month and still get an allowance for). Or I can solve two problems at once or finish a trig test in half the normal amount of time.

Well, that morning in school my brain was functioning on *three* levels. Santa hat firmly in place on my head, I sang "Deck the Halls" with all my heart while simultaneously working to figure out how to save Christmas *and* listening to Turk Martin and his buddies whispering behind my back. I knew the rumors were already flying about my mall escapade and my time in jail, but I didn't care. All that mattered now was the fact that I had been visited by Santa. And Santa was counting on me to make Christmas right again.

The only problem was, I had no idea where to begin.

Mr. McDaniel raised his hand as we held the last note, then closed it into a fist with a flourish to cut us off.

"Very nice!" he exclaimed, his bright eyes falling on me. "It's good to see that you have all regained your enthusiasm this morning." He smiled slightly and I knew he was talking mainly to me. I hadn't exactly been into singing carols lately and I'm sure Mr. McDaniel was starting to wonder if I would ever snap out of it. I knew he was glad to have me back.

"I think everyone deserves a water break," McDaniel said. "Back in five!"

The room exploded with chattering voices as half the choir streamed toward the hallway and the water fountain. Mr. McDaniel disappeared into his office and I walked over to the windows at the back of the room to look out over the gray parking lot and the grayer sky. There was snow in the air—I could smell it. I smiled and crossed my arms over my chest. A white pre-Christmas would definitely be a good start to putting this holiday season back on the right track.

"So, dude, is it true?"

My heart jumped, but I managed not to have a blatantly physical reaction to the fact that Turk and Randy had somehow snuck up on me. I turned to them slowly and smiled.

"Is what true?" I asked, as if I didn't know what they were talking about.

"Did you really spend last night in *jail*?" Randy asked, his whole triangular face crinkling up in disbelief.

"Yeah," I said simply. "I did."

Turk rolled back his shoulders and brought himself up to his intimidating full height, which was even taller than usual since his hair was spiked extra high this morning. He eyed me skeptically. "Whadja do, go for a joyride on too much fruitcake?" he asked.

"Actually, my friends and I tried to burn down the mall," I said, holding Turk's gaze. Okay, so maybe I wasn't in on it. And maybe I didn't want to be found guilty of being in on it. But I had to see their reactions, right?

Turk's and Randy's eyes seemed to take on this whole new expression I'd never seen there before. Could it be . . . respect? Turk's gaze slowly traveled up to the furry brim of my Santa hat and rested there for a moment.

"Wow, man," he said finally. "You're even crazier than I thought."

He pulled up his hand and I almost flinched before I realized he wanted to slap hands with me. I put out my arm tentatively and he brought his hand down on my mine, clasped my fingers for a second, then smiled.

"Crazy," he told me, shaking his head.

After that I had to concentrate to keep from smiling and betraying my giddiness. Suddenly Turk thought I was certifiably cool. All this time all I'd had to do to end the merciless Christmas season teasing was get arrested? Huh.

What the heck was *wrong* with these people?

The door to the hall opened with a creak and the room filled with the sound of girly giggling. I knew it was Sarah and her friends, and I heard my name mentioned a few times, but I didn't give them the satisfaction of acknowledging them. This morning Sarah was wearing yet another Scooby gift—this time a pair of diamond earrings—and I was getting a little sick of seeing her toss her hair around to expose them. Sarah and her heartbreaking ways had sent me down the destructo-path I'd been on, and just being around her today was setting me on edge.

"Hey, Paul," Lainie Lefkowitz said, cutting the giggles short so that everyone could hear. "I see you've got your dorky little hat back."

I looked over my shoulder at her and just stared. I stared and stared and stared as her cocky grin faded, then she had to look away, and then she finally rolled her eyes and *turned* away. I smirked. It was interesting. Suddenly I didn't *care* about the teasing anymore.

But then Sarah had to speak up.

"Yeah, aren't you supposed to stop being Santa when you leave the mall?" she said, earning another round of laughter. "Are you delusional or something?"

That was it. That was all I needed. She just *had* to sink to their level, didn't she? On top of everything else she'd already done to me. All the pent-up tension and anger toward her rushed into my head at once and something inside me snapped. I walked right over to Sarah and her sniveling little friends and the entire room fell silent.

"You had me so fooled," I said, looking right into Sarah's surprised face.

"What?" she asked, trying to laugh it off.

"I thought you really liked me, but it turns out you're nothing but a materialistic, selfish money-grubber. All you were interested in was my car," I said, my whole body heating up.

"What car?" Lainie put in. The laughter was quiet

and less assured this time. I ignored her. My beef was not with Lainie Lefkowitz. It was with the girl who'd tricked me into giving her my heart.

"Well, you know what, Sarah? If you'd rather date a scrawny dorky pseudorapper who sports a monster Adam's apple just because he has money, then that's fine by me," I told her as she tried to look away. "Because I wouldn't touch you again with a ten-foot pole. In fact, you can just take Scooby and all his gifts *and* his stupid homemade rap album and blow them all out your tiny little butt!"

"Oh!" Turk Martin let out as I turned back to take my place on the risers. All the guys hooted and clapped and I even noticed a couple of girls trying to hide their smiles.

Mr. McDaniel walked back into the room and sat down behind the piano.

"Okay, let's try 'Have Yourself a Merry Little Christmas'!" he called out jovially.

Sarah shakily took her place and I could tell she was looking at me from the corner of her eye, but I ignored her. As McDaniel started to play the intro to the song, I saw Turk turn out of the line, perpendicular to everyone else.

I glanced over at him and he grinned and raised his eyebrows. *"Crazy!"* he mouthed, with nothing but admiration in his eyes.

I started to sing. If this was what crazy felt like, I should have tried it sooner.

My mother wanted to drive me to the mall on Tuesday afternoon to turn in my Santa suits, but I convinced her to let me go it alone, giving her some speech about facing the music and being a man. What she didn't know was that I didn't plan to hand in the costumes and walk out of there with my proverbial tail between my legs. All I could think about were Santa's words:

"You can't trust every guy in a Santa suit."

He had to mean Scooby. He just *had* to. But the thing was, I already knew Scooby was a loser and a schemer and a girlfriend stealer. I already knew I couldn't trust him. So what, exactly, was Santa getting at? I was determined to find out.

The glass doors slid open in front of me and I walked into the mall. Dale Dombrowski spotted me from his position at the corner by the Diamond Center and he instantly brought his walkie-talkie to his mouth, his eyes never leaving my face. I knew he was warning the office that I had arrived and I felt a little spear of shame shoot through me. All I had wanted was to be a mall Santa and now I was public enemy number one.

Whatever happened to innocent until proven guilty?

I hopped on the escalator and double-timed it to Papadopoulos's office, more than ready to get this over with. Sharona Drap, Papa-D's secretary, took one look at me, picked up the phone, and started dialing, pretending to be too busy to deal with me. When I walked into the inner office, Mr. Papadopoulos jerked out of his chair, stood up, and smoothed down his tie.

"Paul," he said, clearing his throat. "Didn't think I'd be seeing you again so soon." *Because I figured you'd be well up the river by now,* his eyes added.

My heart twisted, but I reminded myself that I had done nothing wrong. And once I cleared my name, all these people were going to be rushing to apologize to me.

"Just wanted to turn in my costumes," I told him, leaving the neatly stacked pile of red suit pieces on a chair in the corner. They looked so sad and sorry just sitting there. Suddenly I was hit with the realization that I'd never done them justice. My body had been in those suits, but my heart never had. All I wanted was a second chance, but that was never going to happen.

I took a deep breath and looked at my former boss. "For what it's worth, have a merry Christmas," I told him.

His expression softened slightly and his shoulders relaxed. "You too, Paul," he said.

My spirits heavy, I turned and walked back out to the mall. I knew that Dale and Papa-D and everyone in this place would be happy if I would just disappear, but I wasn't ready to leave just yet. I walked across the food court to the bathrooms and made my way to the last stall, my heart pounding with nervousness. I put my backpack on the toilet seat and yanked out my father's trench coat and a fake beard from an old wizard Halloween costume. It took me a while to get everything on, what with my hands shaking and all, but I managed. Finally I pulled my Giants baseball cap low over my head and emerged from the stall.

The mirrors were right across the way and I did a double take when I saw my reflection. Even I didn't recognize myself. I looked like a celebrity who was trying to go Christmas shopping incognito. No one was going to realize who I was in this getup. Not even Scooby.

I slipped from the bathroom with the confidence of a supersleuth, feeling like I could go anywhere and do anything undetected . . . and walked right into Melissa Maya.

"Hey! Watch it!" she screeched.

"Oh . . . sorry," I said. Then, hearing my youngish voice, I cleared my throat and tried again. "Sorry, excuse me . . . sorry."

She narrowed her eyes as I scurried away, but I was pretty sure she didn't recognize me. Still, I was going to have to remember that even in disguise, I wasn't exactly the invisible boy. I stepped onto an escalator behind a crowd of shoppers and tried to blend in.

Moments later I was leaning against one of the pillars across from Santa Land, stewing in a familiar pot of anger. There Scooby sat, in all his Santa glory, welcoming child after child onto his lap, shoving CD after CD into their faces. But other than his normal level of repulsiveness, nothing seemed amiss. After standing there for an hour I started to wonder again what Santa's hint meant. Of course I couldn't trust Scooby, but how was that knowledge going to help me save Christmas? How was it going to help bring my family back together?

Suddenly I missed Holly more than ever. I needed someone to help me figure this out. I needed *her*. But she hadn't even left me her number in Colorado. For all she knew, I had no idea she was there. Maybe I could try calling all the ski lodges in Aspen, looking for her, but even if I found her, wasn't she just going to laugh in my face if I told her how I felt?

"One problem at a time, Paul," I told myself, trying to put all Holly thoughts out of my mind. "Save Christmas first, then deal with finding Holly."

By the time Scooby had sold his tenth CD of the afternoon I was fed up, my stomach was growling, and my beard was itching me something awful. Maybe it was time to lay all this to rest.

But as I walked around the back of Santa Land, I saw something that made me pause. There, behind the collection counter for Hope House, was That Awful Woman. She must have felt me watching her because she looked up from stacking coins and her steely eyes locked with mine. An icy shiver passed down my spine.

I swear on my life, the woman is pure evil.

Finally I managed to drag my eyes away and I kept walking. My disguise must have worked on her because she immediately returned to her business. Knowing her, if she'd recognized me, she would've called out the National Guard. Part of me wanted to just go home and sulk, but I knew instinctively that something was up, so I ducked behind the Stuff 'Em Yourself stocking kiosk to watch her.

On the surface it wasn't that strange, a mall employee volunteering more than once to work the charity booth. But it *was* weird that Marge Horvath was there again. That Awful Woman didn't care about anyone but herself. I figured she spent her free time at home, polishing her broomsticks and counting her money. She definitely wasn't the type to volunteer her time.

Suddenly Marge's head snapped to the right and I followed her gaze to see what had commanded her attention. Eve Elias was stringing up the red rope and telling everyone in line for Santa that it was time for the big guy's dinner break. Marge took note of this, then leaned over to the girl working with her at the charity booth and said something in her ear.

This was it! She was about to do something off—something wrong. I could *feel* it. The girl nodded and Marge smiled her tight smile, grabbed up one of the metal tins full of money, and scurried away toward the escalator.

My mother had told me that when the till reaches eight hundred dollars, the workers always bring the money to the mall office to be put in the safe. My heart sank slightly. Here I thought my instincts had caught Marge in the middle of something devious and I was wrong. So much for my supersleuth career.

But the moment Marge got to the bottom of the escalator, she looked over her shoulder, then ducked *around* it instead. My pulse started to race. Where was she going? What was she doing with all that money?

Forgetting about trying to blend, I took off after Marge, afraid that she'd disappear inside a store or something before I found her again. But when I got to the other side of the escalator, I spotted her in the crowd, making her way back around toward Santa Land.

"Hey, buddy! Watch where you're going!" an angry dad called out as I practically tripped over his stroller. This time I didn't even stop to apologize. I was on to something.

When I came around the second escalator, Santa's throne and the Santa Shack were in full view. Scooby was just walking into the shack from the front door as Marge slipped in through the back! My whole body sizzled with anticipation. Marge and Scooby! Of course! How could I not have seen it before? They'd been together at the mall last night and they were both, well, totally slimy! They were clearly up to something together!

Moving as quietly as I could, I crept up the snowy hills of the North Pole and crawled over to the window in the side of the Santa Shack. I held my breath, turned my baseball cap around, and peeked over the bottom edge of the window. What I saw inside was better than any visions of sugarplums that had ever danced in anyone's head.

Marge and Scooby were divvying up the bills from the charity tin.

"What are you doing?" Scooby demanded, grabbing Marge's bony wrist. "You're taking more than half!"

"That's because you, my little elf, took seventy-five percent last time, remember?" Marge said with a sneer. "To pay for those diamond earrings I got you at discount?"

"Yeah, well, you should've just stolen 'em for me," Scooby said petulantly. "After everything I've done for you . . ."

It took me a moment to snap out of my shock and realize the importance of what I was seeing, but when I did, a devious smile spread slowly from cheek to cheek. At that moment it all fell into place.

It's Beginning to Look a Lot Like Christmas

"DALE! *DALE!*" I STAGE-WHISPERED AS I RUSHED TOWARD the security guard, who was still at his Diamond Center post. I waved at him, trying to get his attention. When his eyes finally fell on me, he planted his legs wide apart and put his hand on his nightstick. His mustache twitched. He looked like a dog sniffing the air for trouble.

"You just stay where you are, friend," he said, holding out his free hand. "Don't come any closer."

"Dale! It's me!" I said desperately, my heart pounding. We were losing precious time. I looked down at my getup and exhaled in frustration. "Look!" I said, pulling down my beard. "It's me, Paul."

Dale's tiny eyes narrowed and he didn't remove his hand from that nightstick. Duh. Why should he? He thought I was a "disturbed teen" who'd tried to burn down the mall.

"Dale, you have to come with me," I said, letting the beard snap back to my chin. (*Ow!*) "There's a crime in the works."

I knew that old-time detective-speak would get his attention. He pressed his lips together and pulled himself up to full height, which wasn't all that impressive.

"Show me," he said.

Moving as quickly as possible, I led Dale up the North Pole hills to the window in the Santa Shack. The glittery fake snow crumbled and shed under our feet, but neither one of us could be bothered with the damage. The moment Dale peeked inside the shack, his face reddened and he started fumbling for his walkie-talkie.

"There's no time for backup," I whispered, grabbing his hand so that he wouldn't make any unnecessary noise. "This bust is all yours, Dombrowski."

His face lit up from the inside and he gazed off past my shoulder. I could just imagine what he was seeing in his mind—commendations, his picture on the front page of the *Record*. This was the kind of glory most mall security guys only dreamed of. With determination in his eyes Dale stood up, walked around to the back door of the Santa Shack, and kicked it in. Okay, it was a little dramatic, but who was I to burst his *NYPD Blue* bubble? I heard Marge yelp and the whole structure shimmied. For a moment I thought it was going to collapse again, but it miraculously held.

"Freeze!" Dale said, pulling out his pepper spray. "I've caught you red-handed!"

I stepped up behind him and smiled at the stunned faces of Marge, who had a few bills sticking out of the low collar of her shirt, and Scooby, who was holding a whole wad of cash in his grubby hand.

"The jig is up, my friends," I said, rubbing my palms together as I grinned. "The jig . . . is . . . up."

Dale had Scooby and Marge stand against the wall while he radioed upstairs for a few of his men to come down. Marge glared at me as we waited, but Scooby, well, Scooby started to cry like a baby without a pacifier. It would have been funny if it hadn't been so darn pathetic.

Three of Dale's deputies appeared and the four of them escorted the criminals up to the mall offices to await the actual police. I waved at them happily as they were led away. It was an utterly perfect moment. My number one enemy and my mom's number one enemy being hauled off to face criminal charges. And it was all because of me . . . and Santa.

Yep, I thought, leaning only half my weight against the precarious Santa Shack. *Christmas is starting to look a whole lot rosier.*

"Mom! Why are those policemen arresting Santa?" a tearful voice squeaked nearby.

My heart dropped and I looked down at the line of kids waiting for Santa's return, all of whom were watching with big, sad eyes as Scooby ascended the escalator. Santa in custody—can you say "traumatizing"? I couldn't believe it. In the midst of my triumph, I'd ruined Christmas for about fifty little kids. Somehow I didn't think this was what Santa had in mind. I had to fix it.

I slipped into the Santa Shack and propped up the fallen door over the opening, then ripped open Scooby's locker, which had been left unlocked in all the commotion. Hanging from one of the hooks was a nice clean spare Santa suit. I said a silent thank-you that Scooby had done at least one thing right in his life.

As I stuffed my arms into the velvety sleeves and buttoned up the fake leather buttons, I could hear the commotion outside growing louder and louder. Most of the kids were wailing and that poor Eve was being accosted by no fewer than six Jersey Mall Moms—plus one Jersey Mall Dad, a rare but dangerously frustrated breed. I glued the beard to my face as quickly as possible, yanked the wig and hat on over my head, and exploded through the front door of the Santa Shack.

"Ho! Ho! Ho!" I shouted, spreading my arms wide. "Merry Christmas!"

The blubbering and screaming stopped. The Jersey Mall Parents' mouths snapped shut. And in that moment, when all hopeful eyes turned to me, I felt a tingling rush that started at my toes and whipped through my body, drawing me up with its warmth and bringing a gleeful smile to my paste-covered face.

The Christmas spirit was back. I was back. And it was good to be me.

"Santa!" a cherubic boy with tears drying on his face shouted. "But . . . but they took you away!"

"Ho ho ho," I chuckled, holding my bowl-full-of-jelly stomach. "No, they didn't, little Timmy—"

Eve's eyebrows shot up.

"Peyton. My name's Peyton," the kid said.

Okay, so maybe I got a little carried away there. The spirit was back, but it hadn't instilled me with Santa's clairvoyance.

"Right, of course, *Peyton*," I replied. "That wasn't me. That was one of my . . . helpers. And it turned out he wasn't such a good guy. Apparently there was a little blip in the whole naughty-and-nice system. But . . . well . . . nobody's perfect, not even Santa, and . . ."

The kids were all staring at me, confused, and Eve

started to wave her hand frantically, telling me to just sit down. I fell into the throne and told myself to shut the heck up and get on with business before I made Santa Claus look like a wack job.

"Okay!" I said. "Who's first?"

Peyton came running up to me and climbed into my lap. He wiped his face with the backs of his pudgy hands and sniffled as he adjusted himself on my thigh. Then he straightened his jacket, folded his hands together, looked right into my eyes, and said, with a seriousness typical of a wizened adult, "Santa, all I want for Christmas is for my sister to get better."

My heart squeezed tightly in my chest and I glanced over at his mother, who was waiting at the bottom of the red carpet. Her hand flew up to cover her heart and I knew she was feeling the same thing I was—a mixture of warm pride and sadness. Any Grinch I had left in me was sent packing at that moment.

I smiled, feeling my eyes crinkle at the edges just like Santa's always did in the drawings in picture books, and put my gloved hand on top of Peyton's head.

"You're a good kid, and your sister is lucky to have you," I told him.

"Thanks, Santa!" Peyton said. Then he pushed himself down, his feet slapped the ground, and he was off and running. He found his mother's hand in the crowd and they walked off together.

"Santa thinks I'm a good kid!" Peyton exclaimed.

"I know! I heard!" his mother replied, doing everything she could to keep from crying. "I happen to agree with him."

I felt like my heart was being pulled out of my

chest toward them and I realized that Peyton had it right. He knew what the spirit of Christmas was about. The giving, the love, the selflessness. That was what I had been missing. How had I gotten through the last few weeks without it?

I grinned and ho-ho-hoed as the next little girl approached me. And as I picked her up to put her on my lap, I promised myself I'd never let anything get in the way of Christmas again. Not ever.

A few hours later my thigh was tingling from all the little bottoms that had jumped onto it and my throat was sore and dry from all the chuckling and talking, but I couldn't have been happier. The mall was about to close and things were winding down when I saw my mother smiling at me from the exact same spot where I'd stood earlier, watching Scooby. It seemed like eons ago.

"Merry Christmas!" I called out one last time, standing and waving after my last lap crawler as he scurried off. Eve strung the red rope across the entrance and walked over to me.

"Nice job, Paul," she said, sliding her green cap from her head. "You really saved me here today."

"Yeah, well, I didn't do it for you," I said.

"Thanks," she replied sarcastically, but with a smile.

"No! I mean . . ." I looked out at the empty space where the line used to be and Eve followed my gaze. I was too exhausted to put what I was thinking into words.

"I know," she said finally. "You did it for them."

"Yeah," I said. "Exactly."

"Well, I hope I see you around," Eve said, starting into the Santa Shack. "I mean, I hope you don't end up locked up in a prison cell with some overgrown beauty queen named Bubba."

I laughed. "Thanks," I said. "Right back at ya."

I loped down the red carpet to my mother, who pushed herself away from her pillar. She was still smiling, but up close I could see that the smile wasn't just about me potentially getting my Santa job back. She had good news. I could taste it.

"What's up?" I asked, unbuttoning the Santa coat and letting in some air.

"Well, thanks to you, I hear, That Awful Woman confessed to skimming money from the registers!" my mother announced, her face all aglow. She looked about fifteen years younger than she had last night at the police station.

"You're kidding!" I exclaimed, realization washing over me. "No wonder she didn't think it was you!"

"Yep! Because she knew it was her!" my mother said with a laugh. "Anyway, Mr. Steiger called me and apologized and asked me to come in, so I did and—"

"He rehired you?" I asked, grasping her elbows. She grasped mine right back.

"Not only that, he made me assistant manager!" my mother exclaimed, practically shrieking.

"No way!" I said, my mind reeling. No more lame reindeer outfit! No more handing out spicy sausages and cheese! My mother grabbed me up in a hug and even though there were still people milling around the mall, I hugged her back, right there in public.

"But wait, it gets even better," my mother told me as I put my arm around her shoulders and we headed back up the red carpet to get my clothes from the Santa Shack.

"What else?" I asked.

"Your father's coming home tomorrow night," she told me, happy tears shining in her eyes. "They say he's made a lot of progress and he can't wait to get home!"

I paused in front of the Santa Shack and looked down at my shiny black boots. I immediately remembered the real Santa's shoes and how scuffed and worn they were. I felt that old, familiar heaviness of guilt start to weigh down on me. I didn't deserve a visit from Santa. Not after the way I'd treated everyone around me.

"Paul? What's wrong? I know a lot has gone on the past few days, but I thought you'd be happy," my mother said, searching my face.

"I know. And I am," I replied. "It's just . . . I don't want Dad to hate me."

"Oh, Paul, your father could never hate you. He loves you," my mother replied, reaching up to touch my face and grabbing my synthetic beard. "We both do."

My heart constricted. After everything I'd done . . . I had no idea what to say.

"I just wish there was something I could do to—"

And then it hit me. The one thing I could do to make my father happy, to prove that nothing had changed, to show everyone that I was back in the spirit of the season. Why hadn't I thought of it before? Santa Claus had already shown me the way.

"Mom?" I said, lifting one corner of my mouth. "Can I stay home from school tomorrow?"

"Why?" she asked slowly, suspiciously narrowing her eyes.

"I have a really, *really* good reason," I promised her.

"And that is?" she prompted.

"You'll see," I said with a grin. "Everyone will see."

I paced across the living room, then back over to the window, looked out, then paced across the living room again and back. I sat down. I stood up. I paced. I picked up a glass ball that had fallen from the tree, tried to fasten it to a branch, and found I couldn't get my fingers to work. Then I sat down again. Stood up again. Looked out the window.

There was nothing on the street. Not a car, not a bike, not a sound. And then something hit the windowpane in front of me. A small, minuscule dot of water. Then another. Then another. There was a low, pleasant hissing as a Honda Civic slipped by and I looked up at one of the streetlights to better see, holding my breath with hope.

And there it was. Snow. Tentative and swirly at first, but then coming faster and thickening. I stood there, mesmerized, watching as the bushes in old Mrs. Gillus's yard were coated in white, as the grass on the front lawn iced over and grew crunchy, as the windshield of my dad's car disappeared. I have no idea how long I watched, but by the time the headlights of my mother's car flashed through the window, I was no longer nervous.

"Dad," I whispered.

I hooked the glass ball onto the nearest tree branch and ran for the door. My father was slowly emerging from the car with my mother's help. She slammed the door and I flicked on the light switch that controlled the outside lights. The whole world seemed to illuminate and I watched from the foyer window as my father's face lit up with joy. My heart overflowed and I knew. I had done the right thing.

I opened the door and walked out, my hands in the pockets of my dark green cords. My boots made wet footprints in the new sheen of snow on the front walk as I joined my parents and turned to look up at our house. And at the Santa in Space light display in all its cheesy, over-the-top Christmas glory.

"How did you do it?" my father asked, gazing at Santa's spaceship, dumbfounded.

"Worked all day," I told him over the lump in my throat. "Plus I had some pretty good blueprints to follow."

I glanced at my mother, who smiled proudly at me, then looked at my father. He couldn't have been more emotional if I'd told him he was going to the Lumberjacking Finals in Minnesota next year.

"Welcome home, Dad," I said, wrapping him up in a hug and patting his back a couple of times.

When I pulled back, my father clasped my shoulders as hard as he could with his weakened hands. "Thanks, son," he said tearfully. "It's going to be a magical Christmas after all."

I'll Be Home for Christmas

"PAUL NICHOLAS! YOU ARE A WONDER!"

Ms. Reginald, the director of Hope House, hadn't stopped singing my praises all night. Well, actually, shouting them over the high volume of the stereo that was currently blaring "Jingle Bell Rock." Not that I could blame her, though. My parents and I, along with a couple dozen employees from the mall, had done a seriously killer job on the annual Hope House Christmas Eve bash.

After Ms. Reginald gave me the hundredth wet, sticky cheek kiss of the evening, I leaned back against the wall of the Hope House rec room and took it all in. Matt and my mom in the center of the ragged carpet, teaching about ten little kids in footsie pajamas how to do the twist. Mall volunteers pouring sodas and fruit punch in the far corner. Marcus handing out cookies and candy. My father sitting at a table with a Hope House volunteer, writing a check for this month's Hope House electric bill. (My dad had strung the lights with his usual disregard for thrift, and when Ms. Reginald expressed her concern about the whirring electric meter in the basement, he offered to foot the bill.)

Turk, Randy, Sarah, and the rest of the choir from school, along with Mr. McDaniel, were gathered around a huge Christmas tree set up in one corner. I'd roped them into singing carols for the kids and McD had jumped at the chance to practice for a live audience. We had already put on our miniconcert and now they were checking out the wrapped presents that local firefighters and police had collected for the kids. The tree was decorated with ornaments made by the children and the walls were papered with their own crayon drawings of Santa and Rudolph and one rather large Christmas jack-o'-lantern that had Christmas lights drawn all over it. I think that artist was a little confused about the holidays, but still, I kinda liked it.

"Whoo! Those kids have no shortage of energy!" my mother said, fanning her face as she walked off the makeshift dance floor.

"I think everyone's having fun," I said, crossing my arms over my chest. "Do you think they're having fun?"

"I do," my mother said, her eyes shining. "And I think that volunteering your time here was a great idea, Paul."

"Thanks," I replied. "I just wish those cops would quit eyeing me like I'm gonna torch the place."

My mother followed my gaze to Officer Pie and his partner, Officer Neville, who were munching on cookies across the room. Officially they had come to represent their precinct, but I couldn't help feeling that they were also here to make sure nothing went awry with the Nicholas kid.

"Well, at least you invited some nice friends and not those hoodlums," my mother said. "It's good for them to see that you don't actually associate with those people."

I bit my lip and looked at her out of the corner of my eye. "Well . . ."

My mother blanched as, always one for perfect timing, Dirk threw open the doors, walked in followed by Ralph, Rudy, and Flora, took one look around, and said:

"Aw, *man*! You tricked us!" Head twitch.

My mother gave me a look that meant business. "What are *they* doing here?"

"I'm out of here!" Flora said, raising her hands.

"Wait!" I called out, rushing over to them and blocking their exit. Ralph stared me down and Rudy did everything he could to keep from looking at me. His foot tapped like crazy and I knew I had about five seconds before they steamrolled me and made a run for it. Not that I could blame them. I'd promised a night of horror movies and prank phone calls and they'd just walked into their version of hell.

"Don't go, you guys," I said, my heart pounding. "Look, I know this isn't your idea of a good time—"

"Not our idea of a good time?" Dirk blurted out. "Paulie! They're playing Bing Crosby!"

"He was the devil," Flora put in, sucking her cheeks. "I mean, have you ever *seen* that *Little Drummer Boy* video with David Bowie? If that doesn't have subliminal kill-kill-kill messages, I don't know what does."

"You guys, give me a chance, okay?" I said. "I've

thought about what you said in jail that night and you were right. If I hadn't been so obsessed with Scooby, we probably wouldn't have gotten caught."

"Exactly," Rudy said.

"But do you realize that if we hadn't gotten caught, you would have *burned down the mall*?" I said this last part under my breath with a wary glance at the officers by the wall. They were watching us intently.

Flora, Dirk, and Rudy exchanged looks. Ralph, of course, continued to stare me down. I felt a glimmer of hope when I saw Dirk's eyes waver.

"Sooner or later someone would have pegged you for the crime and you'd all be facing some serious jail time right now if it wasn't for me. As it is, we're probably just going to get community service and counseling," I said. Then I took a deep breath. "Look, I got a record for you guys," I said. "The least you can do is make it up to me by sticking around and having a piece of cake."

"Cake?" Ralph said, his eyebrows rising.

We all laughed and the tension was broken. Dirk and I gazed at each other. For the first time I felt like we had a mutual understanding and respect.

"Okay, okay!" Dirk said after a long pause. "You're right, Nicholas. You didn't sign on for prison time when you came to us. And we did keep our plans a secret from you."

"Yeah, and we should have thought more about the whole burning down the mall thing," Rudy put in. "I mean, I would have been out of a job!"

I wanted to ask him what he was talking about, but I bit my tongue. I couldn't believe that Radio Shack hadn't fired him after his arrest. But then, there was no telling with those AV guys. Maybe they thought he was even cooler now.

"So where's the cake?" Ralph asked.

Flora rolled her eyes and hooked her arm through Ralph's. "Come on, Doughboy," she said. "Let's get you sugared up."

She tugged him toward the snack table and Rudy followed, his head bobbing as the music switched over to Christina Aguilera's Christmas album.

"So . . . ," I said, once Dirk and I were left alone. "Friends?"

His head twitched and then he smirked. "Yeah, okay," he said. "Friends."

Dirk turned around and joined the party and I felt another stone lift off my shoulders. Everything was slowly falling into place, one problem at a time. As I watched Ms. Reginald dangle mistletoe over the kids by the tree, getting them to kiss each other's cheeks, I saw Sarah break away from the rest of the choir and start across the room toward me, carrying a red gift bag. My pulse skipped ahead with nervous curiosity. We hadn't spoken since the morning I'd gone ballistic on her in choir. Lately I was feeling a bit embarrassed about that, even if she did deserve it.

"Hi, Paul," she said, averting her eyes as she spoke. She was wearing the same red sweater she'd worn the morning I met her, and her hair was pulled back from her perfect face.

"Hey," I said.

"This party is . . . it's really great," she said. She stood next to me and looked out at the room as well, probably to avoid making eye contact.

"Yeah. I'm glad Mr. McDaniel agreed to bring the choir," I said.

"Look," she blurted out suddenly, her face flushing pink as she stared down at the bag in her hands. "I wanted to tell you I broke up with Scooby. And I wanted you to know I had no idea what he was doing." She looked up again. "He told me he made all his money off CD sales. How stupid am I?"

I smiled and didn't refute her claim.

"Anyway, I returned all the presents he bought me," she said, glancing in my direction. "It wasn't right to keep them . . . you know . . . with the way they were bought."

"You returned them?" I asked, surprised. I really looked at her for the first time and saw that her face was full of unabashed hope and honesty. Suddenly I felt warm all over.

"Yeah," she said. "I mean . . . I thought about what you said to me that morning and—"

"I'm really sorry about that," I put in quickly.

"Well, even though I didn't like the way you said it, I realized you were right," Sarah added. She watched the kids as they gathered around the tree at Ms. Reginald's feet. The director started to hand out gifts and as each child received a package, the room seemed to become a little bit lighter with joy. "These kids needed that money more than I needed more stuff."

"Wow," I said, impressed. "That's great, Sarah."

"Well, anyway, I wanted to give this back, too," she said, handing me the gift bag.

Surprised, I looked inside and saw my favorite red wool sweater folded neatly between two sheets of white tissue.

"Thanks," I said.

"You're welcome," she replied. Then she looked up at me tentatively, stood on her toes, and gave me a lingering kiss on the cheek. I waited for the excited tingling sensation to rush over me as it always had when she kissed me, but I felt nothing. Nada. Zilch, zero, zip. Compared to the way kissing Holly felt in my daydreams, Sarah's lips had no effect.

I was officially over her.

Sarah smiled at me sadly and rejoined her friends by the drink table. But I didn't even have time to revel in the sweet irony of the moment. The second Sarah was gone, Officer Pie walked over to me, his notepad out. My heart caught in my throat. What now?

"Paul Nicholas?" he said in a serious voice of doom. My mother and father were at my sides in a flash.

"Yes, Officer?" I said, my throat completely dry.

"I just wanted to let you know that we're dropping all charges against you," Officer Pie said, clearly trying to hold back a smile. "A certain Dirk Evergreen—"

Wait, *Evergreen*?

"—has amended his statement and now claims that you had no knowledge of the arson plot," Pie continued. "And your other friends . . . ah . . . *witnesses* have confirmed his statement."

I glanced at Dirk, Ralph, Rudy, and Flora, all of whom had paused by the door on their way out, and smiled my thanks. I felt like Charlie Brown after all his friends come and decorate that pathetic little Christmas tree of his. I was so moved that I didn't even call them on the fact that their pockets were obviously stuffed with cookies and cake. They deserved a little Christmas cheer, too.

"Later, Paulie," Dirk mouthed.

And then the Anti-Christmas Underground walked out of my life forever.

"Just try to stay out of trouble from now on, okay, son?" Officer Pie said, snapping his notebook closed as my mother hugged me from behind.

"I will, Officer," I said, watching the empty doorway. "I definitely will."

My eyes opened slowly at first, lazily, blinking back the sweet dreams that filled my groggy head. In the darkness my eyes found the clock. It was 4:32 A.M. Christmas Day. I pulled the covers more tightly up to my chin. The windowpanes were lined with frost; the air coming through the tiny crack I'd left open was crisp and fresh. I could feel the excitement rush from my toes all the way to my fingertips. It was Christmas. It had come after all.

Normally I would lie in my bed wide awake, counting the seconds until it was time to throw the Muppets Christmas CD on my stereo and crank it up to wake my parents. But this wasn't a normal Christmas and I couldn't wait a second longer to welcome it. I threw aside my covers and ran downstairs, not even trying to stay quiet.

I came around the corner and slid into the living room, where the tree was fully lit up. There weren't many packages this year, but I wasn't expecting many. I knew my parents were strapped for cash and I wasn't sure if Santa would be stopping by this year, after everything I'd done. I fell on my knees and searched for my name on box after box. Finally, practically trembling with anticipation, I found one—a small one—with my name written on it in big block letters.

Holding my breath, I slid the top off the red-and-white-striped box, and I think I almost fainted. There, sitting on a bed of white cotton, was a single silver key with a black rubber knob. And across the knob in silver letters was written one beautiful word:

Jeep.

I dropped the box and ran outside, my bare feet slipping in the new blanket of snow. Sitting in my driveway was a pristine red Jeep Cherokee, definitely a previously owned model, but mine nonetheless. I walked over to it, placed my hands on the side window, and peered through the glass. Black leather interior, floor mats only slightly worn, pine-scented fir tree dangling from the rearview mirror.

My parents were the greatest.

I turned and walked slowly into the house to put the key back in its box so that I could open it all over again when my parents woke up. Maybe I would just let them sleep this year. They'd been through enough. And I could wait till . . . oh . . . six o'clock or so.

I smiled as I closed the door behind me. But even though I'd gotten the Jeep I'd been hoping for and even though the house was back to normal and my parents were happy and safe upstairs, I still felt like Christmas was not going to be complete.

There would be no grudging noontime call from Holly to find out what I'd gotten. There would be no day-after-Christmas get-together with her to have a noncelebratory pizza. There would be no looking into Holly's mocking eyes as she teased me over my post-Christmas rundown.

I knelt down under the tree and replaced the key with a sigh. I was just thinking about dragging myself back to bed when I heard on the roof the prancing and pawing of each little hoof. I stood up, my heart pounding, and suddenly Santa fell from the chimney into my fireplace, kicking up a cloud of soot.

"Santa!" I whispered.

He pulled himself up and dusted himself off, then dragged his sack out behind him. "Merry Christmas, Paul," he said with a wink. "Thought I'd save the best house for last!"

"Wow," I said, staggering back a few feet from the tree as he started to unpack his gifts. "I . . . I wasn't sure if you were coming."

"Oh, Paul, you knew I'd be here," Santa said as he placed a sizable box under the tree. He stood up and patted his hands against his legs, then looked down at his cracked, dirty boots. "Too bad you didn't get to see me at the start of the night, though. Mama had those boots gleaming."

"I'm sure she did," I said with a smile.

"Well, now," Santa said, picking up one of my mother's fudge bars from the plate on the hearth. "Why the long face? Didn't you get everything back to normal?"

"Almost everything," I replied, tilting my head. "But there's still something missing. . . ."

"Some*one,* you mean," Santa said with a knowing look.

"I still haven't heard from Holly," I admitted.

"Well, Paul, Christmas isn't over yet," Santa said, smiling. "What are you going to do about it?"

I looked at the jolly old elf like he was crazy. What

could I do about it? All I knew was that Holly was somewhere in Aspen. It wasn't like I could just call her up and apologize and ask her to ditch her mother and come home. There was just no way. Unless someone suddenly handed me a Holly LoJack and a plane ticket, I was going to be spending Christmas Holly-free.

"Hmmm . . . ," Santa said, laying a finger aside of his nose. "If only you had some way of locating her. Some . . . magical figure, perhaps, with a psychic knowledge of where all children are at all times around the world. Now . . . where might a boy in need *find* such a creature?"

The grin spread slowly across my face as I looked into Santa's mischievous twinkling eyes.

"Did you say this was your last stop?" I asked him.

"I'm as free as a snowbird," Santa said, widening his arms. He looked up at the ceiling, almost like he was looking *past* it to the roof, and smiled.

"Santa," I said, picking up my jacket from a nearby chair, "I like your style."

Epilogue

THE SUN WAS SHINING HIGH OVER THE MOUNTAINS AS my Jeep's all-terrain tires rumbled over the snow-covered drive in front of Aspen's Rocky Mountain Lodge. I looked up at the huge log cabin, decorated with twinkling white lights and covered in at least ten inches of snow, wondering which window was Holly's. As I slowed the Jeep to a stop, I got my answer. A sliding glass door a couple of stories above me opened and out stepped Holly herself, wearing a red-and-black ski jacket, her hair tumbling over one shoulder. She walked to the wooden railing surrounding her veranda and leaned her elbows on it, staring out across the trees.

My heart stopped when I saw her. Somehow, in that moment, I fell in love at 5,255th sight.

But what was I supposed to do now? How was I going to explain how I'd found her . . . how I'd gotten here? How was I supposed to explain that I'd woken up this morning in New Jersey and shown up just a few hours later more than halfway across the country?

Holly closed her eyes and smiled as a breeze ruffled her hair. Man, she was beautiful. I climbed out of the car and slammed the door. Whatever I was going to say, I couldn't wait to say it any longer.

"Holly!" I called out.

She jumped slightly, then looked down. Her eyes lit up when she saw me and her smile slowly widened. I couldn't have been more relieved. A part of me had still thought she might not be so happy to see me—that she'd instantly start hurling snowballs in my direction.

"Paul?" she said. "What the heck are you doing here?"

But I didn't have time to answer. Holly whirled around and disappeared into her room. I ran up the steps to the lodge and burst through the front door. The lobby was warm and cozy, thanks to the huge fire crackling and hissing in an old-fashioned stone fireplace. A ten-foot-tall tree laced with popcorn and cranberry strands stood in the corner. The entire place was trimmed with evergreen garlands and wreaths, poinsettias and twinkling lights. The scents of burning wood, fir trees, and cinnamon filled the air. It was like a Christmas wonderland.

Suddenly Holly appeared at the top of the wide staircase in her snow jacket and jeans. Our eyes met and she barreled down the steps. For a split second I thought she was going to throw herself into my arms, but she suddenly seemed to remember our fight and she stopped a couple of feet away from me. I could feel the few people who were milling around the lobby watching us. My heart was doing everything it could to make me very aware of its presence.

"What are you doing here?" Holly asked again. She

held the fingertips of one hand with the fingertips of
the other, looking cautious.

"I came here to tell you that—"

I stopped. This was too weird. This was *Holly*!
Could I really tell her what I was thinking? What I was
feeling? Her eyebrows came together as she stared at me.

"Paul?" she said.

This was insane. I hadn't come all this way to say
nothing. I took a few steps closer to her and tried again.

"I came to tell you that—"

Damn. Damn, damn, damn, damn, damn. I couldn't
do it. Not with her looking at me with those big green
eyes. It was like she could see *through* me. And then, as
we stood there, something came over her face. It was as if
she suddenly lit up from within. She straightened herself
up and smiled, understanding filling her eyes. I took a
couple of steps closer.

"No fair not finishing a sentence, Nicholas," she
said lightly. "You're breaking the Pact."

My heart was slamming around in my chest and I
started to sweat. There was so much to say and I
couldn't find a single word. All I wanted to do was . . .

And then I saw it. It was like somebody had put it
there on purpose, anticipating my inability to articu-
late everything going on inside—my inability to make
my move. It was exactly the motivation I needed.

Mistletoe.

Holly opened her mouth to speak, but I stopped
her with a kiss. I slid my hands under her soft hair and
pressed my lips to hers and time just stopped. For a
split second Holly didn't move and I was petrified.
Any second she was going to push me away and laugh

in my face. But then I felt her hands on my back and I felt her pulling me closer to her and I smiled even as we kept kissing.

In that moment I realized I had done it. I had everything I wanted. It was Christmas and my father was okay and my mother had a new job and my house was fixed and Marge and Scooby had been caught and I . . . well . . . I was kissing the girl I loved. The girl I really, truly loved.

When we finally broke apart, we both smiled and I hugged her close to me, burying my face in her hair. Holly started to laugh and then I did, too. We had kissed, but we were still us. And as I stood there in the middle of a killer ski lodge in the middle of Aspen, Colorado, holding my best friend in the world, I swear I heard the sound of jingle bells jingling and a deep voice exclaim from somewhere out of sight,

"Merry Christmas to all, and to all a good night!"